THE DENDROLOGIST AND OTHER STORIES

BY

JAMES W. POINDEXTER

This is a work of fiction. Names, characters, places, and incidents either are the product of the author's imagination or are used fictitiously, and any resemblance to actual persons, living or dead, business establishments, events, or locales is entirely coincidental. Although some historical names, dates and information are used, such names, dates and information have not been verified and may not be accurate.

To

Sarah,

Emeigh,

Wade and Elizabeth,

Liz and Alec and Ethan

Will and Christina, Remy and Rocco

And special thanks to

Writer's Bloc Friends

Ray, Mark, Dan and Jamie

And to

Brian Crawford

And finally, gratitude to

Richard Baxman

for towing my car back from the East Coast and

many adventures along the way.

Contents

THE DENDROLOGIST

James W. Poindexter

Johnny Filbert sat under a redwood tree, his back against the trunk's spongy cushion of bark. It was a warm and sunny morning. The buzzing of insects blended with the happy shouts of children from a nearby school.

Johnny was thirty-one years old, although he appeared older. His face was creased and worn. His muscular arms, adorned with tattoos, were folded across his chest. They were not the arms of a man who had enjoyed a life of comfort.

He stared up through the branches. His grandfather had planted the trees decades earlier. The quarter-acre yard behind the San Anselmo cottage had grown into a small forest.

His grandfather's journal rested on his lap. The original cover had worn away long ago from a combination of sweat, dirt and hard use. Two pieces of plywood now held the journal together. The front cover was simply titled, *Observations of Trees by Aloysius Dendro Filbert.*

According to Johnny's grandfather, *Aloysius* (pronounced *aloe - ISHIS*) meant *famous warrior*. It was the Latin version of the more common names Louis, Luigi or Luis. "My father wanted a brawny athlete," his grandfather had said, "and all he got was a scrawny bookworm. But what do you expect with a name like *Aloysius*?"

Dendro, he had explained, was Greek for *tree* and *Filbert* was a kind of *nut.*

His grandfather had became a warrior of sorts, but not in the way anybody expected. As a plant biologist, he devoted his life to the study of *trees.* He often spoke at public hearings, urging the protection of trees which stood in the path of human progress. "So you see, Johnny," his grandfather had said, "*Aloysius Dendro Filbert* does make sense. I'm a *warrior* and a *tree nut* and that's a pretty fair description of what I've been doing the past fifty years."

As a boy, Johnny frequently visited his grandfather in San Anselmo. The town was picturesque, located in wooded Ross Valley on the northeast side of Mt. Tamalpais, just across the Golden Gate Bridge from San Francisco. Back then, they explored the wooded terrain on foot, hiking nearly every path and fire road.

One day, they walked all the way from San Anselmo to Stinson Beach. After eighteen miles, they were tired and collapsed on the sand, watching surfers ride the frothy waves and seagulls glide overhead. They shared a beer, even though Johnny was barely twelve at the time. "The beach is nice, Johnny," his grandfather had said, "but I couldn't live here. Not enough trees."

They took the bus from the beach back to San Anselmo, along Sir Francis Drake Boulevard. The road was named for Queen Elizabeth I's favorite pirate, who had reportedly visited the coast in 1579, plundering Spanish galleons and trading with the local Miwok.

During Johnny's childhood, he and his grandfather were inseparable. Later, however, their relationship soured. The reasons were fairly simple. Johnny dropped out of college and took a job as caretaker on a pot farm in Humboldt County. One day, there was a gun fight. The cartel tried to run Johnny off the land. One of the attackers was wounded. Johnny went to prison for two years for assault with a deadly weapon. Most people, including the sentencing judge, felt Johnny had been mostly acting in self-defense.

As a result of these events, his grandfather was disappointed and Johnny was angry. Like fighters in the ring, they withdrew to their corners, nursing their wounds.

After prison, Johnny worked odd jobs. His parents had died while he was in prison. So, he and his grandfather were all that remained of the family. It was probably inevitable that they should reunite. They began exchanging birthday cards and occasional phone calls.

Years had passed. Johnny was now back in San Anselmo, not to visit his grandfather, but to bury him. However, there would be no *actual* burial nor any formal service or interment. In fact, there was no body over which rites might be performed.

Five years ago, his grandfather had disappeared.

The only proceedings marking his grandfather's *passing* would take place that afternoon, in a courtroom. Johnny was very familiar with the applicable laws, in particular, California Probate Code, Section 12401 which stated: "… *a person who has not been seen or heard from for a continuous period of five years by those who are likely to have seen or heard from that person, and whose absence is not satisfactorily explained after diligent search or inquiry, is presumed to be dead.*"

Obviously, *presumed dead* was a far cry from *actually dead,* yet the presumption of death was enough to trigger the laws of succession and allow an estate to be admitted to probate.

Five years after his grandfather's disappearance, Johnny had hired a lawyer, who filed a petition to establish the grandfather's *presumed* death.

Nobody was really surprised that his grandfather might have wandered off or even committed suicide. In his later years, the old man suffered from debilitating arthritis. A part time caregiver visited him three days a week for a period of time but was no longer working for him at the time of the disappearance.

The court hearing that afternoon was, for the most part, uneventful. Johnny was the main witness.

"Tell us about your grandfather's family," his attorney asked.

"Well, he only had me," Johnny said, "since his only child, my mother, died years ago. He wasn't married and he had no brothers or sisters. His parents were long gone. So, like I said, there was just me."

"When was your last contact?"

"Oh, that would be the year before he went missing. He sent me a birthday card and then I called him on the phone. We talked for a while."

"How did you find out he was missing?"

"A neighbor called me. He had my number. He said my grandfather was missing and thought I should know about it."

"And, did you return to San Anselmo?"

"Yes, it was soon after my grandfather's disappearance. I came back to San Anselmo and stayed for a while at my grandfather's house."

"What did you do?"

"Well, I made a police report. When he didn't return, I arranged with you to get a power of attorney so I could manage my grandfather's property in his absence. I rented out the house and spent most of the past five years traveling."

"Who did you work with at the police?"

"It was Detective Fresa. She took the report and did whatever investigation she thought was necessary."

"What did Detective Fresa do?"

"Not much."

"How about you? Did you try to find your grandfather?"

"Yes. I hired a private investigator, Mr. Archer. "

Investigator Archer also testified at the hearing.

"Mr. Archer, what efforts did you make to find Aloysius Filbert?" the attorney asked.

"I made the usual database searches, looked for any bank or credit activity and made in-person inquiries to various people in the neighborhood who had known him."

"And what did you find?"

"Nobody had seen him. There were no credit or bank transactions over the past five years."

A neighbor also testified, confirming that the grandfather had suffered from arthritis and the approximate date he had gone missing.

The hearing had one tense moment. The judge asked if any witnesses wished to testify against Johnny's petition. Detective Fresa stepped forward.

"What do you wish to add, Detective?" the judge asked.

Detective Fresa described her investigation. "It's an unusual case. People don't simply disappear. This wasn't an alien abduction. Normally, there's a witness. You find a car or a wallet or a credit card receipt. Here, the man simply vanished."

"Do you have any proof of *foul play*?"

Detective Fresa shook her head. "No, your honor, only suspicions. Johnny Filbert, the grandson, has a criminal record. It seems pretty obvious. He needed money and he was the sole heir."

The judge was unimpressed. "Look, you've had five years to assemble any evidence relevant to this inquiry. I'm not going to hold up the estate over speculation. Do you have anything else to say, Detective?"

"No, your honor," she said, plainly embarrassed by the judge's rebuke.

The hearing ended with the judge ruling in Johnny's favor. His grandfather was legally *presumed dead* and the estate could proceed to probate.

Johnny's grandfather had left a one-page, handwritten will, which designated Johnny as the executor and said: "*I leave my home in San Anselmo, all my possessions, including my laboratory equipment and journals, to my sole heir and grandson Johnny Filbert /s/.*"

Following the hearing, Johnny's attorney submitted the will and the court's order to the probate department. The attorney was optimistic that the court would soon award the estate to Johnny.

By day's end, Johnny felt at ease. His troubles would soon be over.

The next morning, Johnny was again sitting under the redwood tree, paging through his grandfather's journal. He had read it before but it was pretty dense. *Observations of Trees by Aloysius Dendro Filbert* bulged with data, botanical drawings, pressed leaves, seed collections, lab notes and articles. The overarching theme was the science of trees.

The journal's first half was like a biology textbook, with headings such as:

- Redwood (Sequoia sempervirens), a mechanism for absorption of air-borne water molecules,
- Joshua Tree (Yucca brevifolia), defenses to ultraviolet radiation,
- Carbon Reduction Inhibitors in Sierra Foothill Forests.

The second half of the journal was less scientific, almost poetic, a sort of ode to trees. For example, one part was dedicated to the story of Tristan and Isolde, the star-crossed lovers who, reunited in death, emerged from their graves as two trees, their branches intertwined and inseparable.

There were references to Greek myths, including the story of Daphne who, weary from Apollo's advances, was transformed into a laurel tree. There were also numerous drawings including a drawing of Sylvanus, the Roman god of woods and uncultivated lands.

Johnny was not sure what prompted the change in tone between the first and second parts of the journal. He suspected it had something to do with his grandfather's close encounter with the most ancient of trees, the Bristlecone Pine *(Pinus longaeva)*.

Johnny recalled, years earlier, asking his grandfather, "What's the oldest tree you ever saw?"

His grandfather had pursed his lips, thinking back. "Well, there was the Bristlecone Pine known as the *Prometheus Tree* which grew near Wheeler Peak in Nevada."

"Who was Prometheus?"

"Another good question. He was an ancient Greek god, a Titan, who created the first humans out of mud. So he was really, really old!"

"So, how old was the tree?"

"Five thousand years old. Unfortunately, back in 1965, it was cut down. At the time, it was the world's oldest living thing. Two hundred generations of people had come and gone during that tree's lifetime."

Johnny had asked for details. "Why'd they cut it down?"

His grandfather was a patient man, and didn't mind all the questions, especially from his grandson. "It was sad. A geography student from the University of North Carolina was responsible. He wanted to determine the Prometheus Tree's age, but the usual, non-fatal method of coring didn't work. So, he decided to cut down the tree and count the rings."

"Grandpa, why do you know so much about the Bristlecones?"

"Well, I was part of a scientific team to study the fallen Prometheus Tree. And that work led to a multi-year contract with the U. S. Forest Service. We did months of research at the Ancient Bristlecone Pine Forest on the eastern edge of California."

"Were there old trees there?"

"Oh yes," his grandfather replied in a reverential tone. "That's where I met the *Methuselah Tree.* It's nearly five thousand years old."

After the Prometheus incident, the Methuselah Tree's location was a closely guarded secret. His grandfather, however, was able to spend months living in the Bristlecone Forest. "Night after night," he wrote in his journal, "I slept next to Methuselah, staring up through its gnarled and twisting branches at the star-filled sky."

Johnny felt his eyes closing. The sweet late morning air and the cadence of insect sounds and children's voices made a tranquilizing elixir.

The backyard gate suddenly creaked open. "Excuse me, Johnny," a woman's voice called out.

Johnny sat up. “Who’s there?”

“It’s Detective Fresa. Just have a couple questions for you.”

By then, Johnny was on his feet, walking toward the gate, holding the journal tightly under his right arm. “C’mon, Detective. I have nothing to say to you.”

“You don’t want to impede my investigation, do you?”

“What investigation! You’ve had five years to find my grandfather and, as far as I can tell, you’ve made no progress.”

“Well, you can’t find someone who isn’t there,” she said, sounding defensive.

“Look, I’m done helping you,” he countered. “Like the judge said, you only have speculation. If you need anything, call my lawyer.”

She shrugged. “Just remember, Johnny, I haven’t given up. I’d hate to see you do more jail time.”

“Whatever!” he replied, waving her off.

After dinner, Johnny reviewed his grandfather’s recent bank statements. The balances were ample. His grandfather had been frugal and Johnny, if he were careful, would not have to worry about money again, assuming the probate court accepted the will and gave its approval.

He lit a fire in the fireplace, then sat in his grandfather’s favorite rocker. He picked up the journal and began reading where he’d left off. The question which seemed to preoccupy his grandfather was: *why do trees, particularly ancient trees like Bristlecone Pines and Sequoias, never age?*

There were several entries on the topic of cellular *senescence*. Some cells stopped replicating and died, while others did not. The question was, why?

Johnny remembered learning about *senescence* from his grandfather. He knew from school that plants and animals were composed of cells, that a cell's nucleus contained spiraling molecules of DNA, and that each cell would periodically replicate itself through mitosis.

"The human body," his grandfather had said, "is made up of over 30 trillion cells, which are constantly being replaced. But cells don't live forever, Johnny. A cell, which can no longer replicate itself, is *senescent*. It's a natural part of the aging process. Normal cells divide, senescent cells die or, if they remain active, can cause disease."

His grandfather devoted long passages in his journal to the topic of aging. "Why should people die at seventy or eighty, while some clams live into their hundreds and Bristlecones live for thousands of years?"

All creatures were composed of cells, but their life spans varied wildly.

When talking about the ancient trees, one also had to distinguish between *clonal* and *individual* life spans. Bristlecone pines were the oldest *individual* living things, but some *clonal* species were even older. A clonal species was one that reproduced itself from the same genetic material, such as roots or rhizomes.

A creosote bush in the Mojave Desert, known as the *King Clone,* was believed to be *eleven thousand years old*. Aspens were also a clonal species which sprouted from the same root system. The *Pando* grove in Utah was believed to be eighty thousand years old.

Johnny tried to imagine himself living a thousand years. Some people he'd known had grown tired of life after only a couple decades. Life's bullshit wore them down.

What wisdom could a thousand year old human impart to younger generations? Johnny assumed the advice would be more profound than the modern litany of *get A's, go to Harvard, make money, get married, exercise* and *eat vegetables*. He tried to imagine a happy couple celebrating their 900th anniversary. The speeches could drag on for days, recounting the couple's memorable moments.

The idea of ancient humans roaming the earth was almost comical. Unlike trees, which produced little waste (except for oxygen and soil enriching compost), people, particularly thousand year old people, would likely leave a rather toxic footprint.

Once, hiking with his grandfather, Johnny had seen a sign by the trail that said, *Leave No Trace*. Someone had left an empty beer can on top of the sign. That had summed it up. People could be interesting, but they probably were not mature enough to live as long as trees. *Perhaps,* he thought, *a species' longevity should depend on its contribution to the health of the planet.*

Everything, according to his grandfather, was always in a process of *aging*. Things came with an expiration date. It was as if a mad scientist had endowed each species with its own random time clock.

Tucked between pages of his grandfather's journal was an abstract from the National Institutes of Health about *senescence* in Bristlecone Pines:

> ***"We evaluated hypotheses of senescence in old trees by comparing putative biomarkers of aging in the***

> ***Great Basin bristlecone pine (Pinus longaeva) ranging in age from 23 to 4713 years****. To test a hypothesis that water and nutrient conduction is impaired in old trees we examined cambial products in the xylem and phloem. We found no statistically significant age-related changes....The hypothesis of continuously declining annual shoot growth increments was tested... No statistically significant age-related differences were found. The hypothesis that aging results from accumulation of deleterious mutations was addressed...None of these parameters had a statistically significant relationship to tree age. It appears that the great longevity attained by some ... bristlecone pines is unaccompanied by deterioration of meristem functor in embryos, seedlings, or mature trees, ...* ***We conclude that the concept of senescence does not apply to these trees****.*"

Tree cells that never age! For his grandfather, that was something magical, akin to a medieval talisman, capable of turning slag into gold. His grandfather wanted to know: *Why should a tree live a hundred times longer than humans*?

Human biology, he concluded, was inherently flawed. All kinds of forces could cause *senescence* in human cells. There were internal causes such as the erosion of DNA due to the wear and tear of constant replication and external causes such as ultra-violet radiation.

His grandfather had written, "People don't die as a whole. Instead, individual cells become senescent and eventually destroy one or more critical functions." By comparison, trees were nearly indestructible. "You can cut off their limbs and subject them to wind, ice, fire and lightning, yet they cling to life. Give them sun, water and a few nutrients and they can live forever."

These ideas led to experiments, which began in earnest ten years before his grandfather's disappearance. That was when his grandfather started combining human and plant DNA.

Other researchers had attempted to create a hybrid plant and human cell. The pharmaceutical companies were always looking for breakthroughs in the fight against disease. Those were heady times, like the search for the fountain of youth.

His grandfather, however, focused on DNA from three sources: tree roots, common fungi and human tissue. Although human and tree cells were generally incompatible, they did share a compatibility with a certain type of fungus known as *mycorrhizae fungi*. His grandfather had written, "Could using fungus as a medium provide a space for interactive bonding between human and tree cells?"

Johnny yawned. It was 10 p.m. He put aside the journal after reading all but the final ten pages. That final section contained the secrets, the ones which could still send him back to jail.

He stirred the remains of the fire and finished a glass of his grandfather's prickly pear wine. It was a little syrupy, but not too bad.

Johnny woke early the next morning. He felt refreshed and almost optimistic. It was an odd feeling for someone so accustomed to failure.

He could see the trees through the kitchen window. The dewy leaves sparkled in the morning sun. *What if humans could synthesize energy from the sun like plants?* Maybe he was starting to think like his grandfather.

Johnny's phone rang.

"Hello?"

It was his attorney. "Johnny, that detective, Olivia Fresa…"

"What about her?"

"She got a warrant. They're on their way to the house."

"Shit!" Johnny shouted and hung up.

He found his grandfather's journal in the living room where he'd left it. Without hesitating, he found a knife and used it to cut out the journal's final ten pages. He threw the pages into the still smoldering fireplace where, after a minute, they burst into flames. He placed the journal on a book shelf near some old photo albums, then dashed from room to room, straightening up what he could.

Two patrol cars arrived. Detective Fresa knocked forcefully. Johnny opened the front door. The detective stood there, accompanied by three other officers.

"Here's a search warrant, Johnny," she said, handing him the document. "You should know that one of the neighbors finally talked. Now that you're claiming your grandfather's estate, it got him thinking. He remembers you returning right *before* your grandfather's disappearance. You're the only link to his final days."

Johnny stood there, trying to remain expressionless.

Two officers walked into the backyard and began sweeping the area with ground-penetrating radar and a metal detector. Detective Fresa and another officer searched the house.

Johnny walked unsteadily to the kitchen and sat at the table. He remained there, nervously tapping his foot, wondering what to do.

This won't end well, he thought. His grandfather had done so much for him, even given him the house. It was all about to come out.

Johnny chided himself. He had become complacent. For years, Detective Fresa had been indifferent about the case. Finding a missing old man was not her priority. But now, her interest had been piqued, egged on by the judge's criticism and the neighbor's assertion that Johnny had visited before the disappearance.

It was foolish to assume the truth would not be revealed. Everybody had secrets. Johnny had tried to lock his away. But, as his grandfather had said, "Secrets are like rats trapped in an attic; they scrape and gnaw until they find a way out."

The police search went on for hours. Johnny could hear Detective Fresa and her partner, chatting, going room to room. They weren't showing much interest in their work. On the other hand, the two cops in the back yard were animated. They had marked off a grid, and were using their equipment to probe the ground, a square foot at a time.

One of the outdoor cops suddenly yelled, "Got a hit!"

"Yeah," confirmed the other cop, "something here."

Johnny jumped up and peered out the kitchen window. He saw the two cops pick up shovels and start digging.

Detective Fresa and her partner walked outside to join the others. After a quarter hour of digging, one of the cops stooped down and reached into the hole. His hand emerged holding a piece of metal. "Damn!," he said, angrily. He held it out to the others. "It says *Camby.*"

Johnny sighed, feeling momentary relief. It was a dog tag, apparently from his grandfather's old hound, Cambium, whom everyone had called Camby.

The search continued into the afternoon. Finally, as the officers were preparing to leave, Detective Fresa approached Johnny in the kitchen. She handed him the bank statements. “Don’t count your money too soon, Johnny.”

Johnny just stared at her, too weary to say anything.

Johnny sat in the kitchen for another hour, not sure what to do. Had they really searched the *whole* yard? It made no sense. His curiosity was overwhelming his better judgment. He needed to know.

He took a shovel from the garage and walked to the back yard. It was late afternoon The redwood tree, where he had been sitting the day before, was now deep in shadow.

He looked nervously around him, half expecting to find somebody watching. It was quiet. He stuck the shovel into the ground at the base of the redwood, and started digging, slowly at first, then faster.

Like most trees, redwood roots were in the top few feet of soil. After an hour, Johnny had dug a large hole nearly three feet deep. He kneeled, plunging both arms into the hole. Suddenly, he felt it. He shined a light from his phone.

He saw the rough shape of a body, but it was … different.

No wonder, he thought, *the police failed to discover it*. The body, from finger tips to toes, had taken on the texture of wood. It was attached in several places to the tree’s roots. The body’s one-time bones, tendons and ligaments were now indistinguishable from the surrounding roots.

Johnny wasn’t sure what he had expected to see. Perhaps a decomposed body, or other evidence that his grandfather’s experiments had failed. "Goddamn, he did it!" Johnny shouted. The experiments had worked, were working.

What remained of his grandfather's body was now a functioning part of the tree's root system, absorbing water, nitrogen, phosphorus and potassium and transmitting them upward into the tree's canopy.

Johnny kneeled there, marveling at the result. His grandfather's once arthritic body had transformed into something vital, useful and alive.

It was getting dark. Johnny shoveled the dirt back into the hole and smoothed it over.

Nobody, except Johnny, had known about the experiments. His grandfather's efforts to transform from *Homo sapiens* to *Sequoia sempervirens* had no doubt been painful, but perhaps no more so than the arthritis slowly killing him.

Detective Fresa had been correct. Johnny did return to San Anselmo several times before his grandfather's *disappearance.* On the final visit, Johnny found his grandfather dead, at least in human form. The transformation had already begun. His grandfather had changed, his skin already resembling the fibrous wood he would become.

His grandfather had left a note on the side table. It instructed Johnny to read the last ten pages from the journal. There, in the final pages of the journal, his grandfather asked to be buried at the foot of the redwood tree, and provided instructions, including illustrations, explaining how to graft his still evolving body to the tree's roots. The process was similar to grafting one tree branch to another, a process Johnny had learned years before from his grandfather.

His grandfather's note concluded with the following: *And Johnny, never tell anyone where I'm buried. They would just want to dig me up. After all, if all goes well, I'm not really dead, simply changed into something better, more permanent and less painful. This will be our little secret.*

In the years that followed, neighbors would see Johnny sitting outdoors, his back to the redwood tree, engaged in conversation, with nobody in particular, except perhaps … the tree.

THE HELIOTROPE

James W. Poindexter

Bear Sargent sat heavy in the saddle. He was a large man, with a dark beard. Given his face and size, he kind of resembled a bear. He wore a Stetson knock-off and a plaid shirt. After eight hours of riding, it was tough to tell where the horse left off and he began. He was only twenty but his body ached like an old geezer's.

"Goddamn, Curly," he said to the man riding nearby, "we've been at it since daybreak. All 'cross these hills. I haven't seen a single sheep in over an hour."

"You heard what Henry said," the other man replied. "He's short twenty head. They got to be someplace."

A McNab shepherd was running in front of them. They called him Bump, because of a benign growth behind his left ear. Like other McNabs, Bump's purpose in life was gathering sheep. He was black and white like a border collie but with short hair. He was fearless and never stopped moving.

Coastal Sonoma in 1969 was sheep country. The temperate climate, vineyards and apple orchards were further inland. By contrast, the coast was a collection of rocky beaches, windswept bluffs, deep ravines and hilly grasslands. It was as wrinkled as your grandpa's face, etched by ocean, wind and rain and fractured by the odd earthquake. Exposed outcroppings had long ago been rubbed smooth by migrating mammoths. What few trees existed, were leaning leeward, as if fleeing the sea.

"This ground ain't much good for nothin' but sheep," Bear said, mostly to himself. It was true. Sheep were comfortable on steep terrain. They were sure-footed and good scroungers. His father had joked, "Your typical sheep could find a blade of grass on a rock wall." Sometimes the sheep were too adventuresome. Bear had seen one fall off a bluff and another slide into a ravine.

"Maybe we should check Alvarez Creek," Bear suggested. The creek was inland and the weather was a bit warmer. The sheep sometimes went there for water.

"There's an idea," Curly agreed. "Fog's movin' in. Pretty soon, we won't see shit.'

The fog was a clock of sorts, like the planetary orbits, the phases of the moon, the tides and the sun. Bear was always conscious of the sun, with its ups and downs, solstices and equinoxes. The sun was the key to it all. It could dictate your mood and, on a grander scale, life on earth.

The coastal fog often blotted out the sun. During summer months, the fog would lift around ten in the morning and reappear at three in the afternoon. Even while inland valleys might be blistering hot, the coast could be thirty degrees cooler.

Most times, the fog was thick and suffocating. It chilled the bones and spurred a heavy heart. In Bear's experience, this fog was nothing like Carl Sandburg's poem:

The Fog

The fog comes
on little cat feet.
It sits looking
over harbor and city
on silent haunches
and then moves on.

Out on the bluffs, the fog came, not on little cat feet, but like a bulldozer. It was brutal and blinding. More to the point, once the fog came, a stray sheep would be invisible in the ashy grayness.

Bear had sometimes lost his bearings in that swirling mist. When it happened, he'd followed the on-shore wind, trusting it to lead him away from the cliffs which dropped straight down to the rocky beach.

The fog had been responsible for hundreds of shipwrecks. Ancient mariners would lose their way, their ships foundering on the rocks. All seafaring people had experienced the peril.

For more than ten thousand years, local tribes had lived on the coast. The Pomo and Miwok used ocean-going canoes for fishing and transport. Bear had imagined their canoes caught in fog, ramming the rocks, tossing paddlers into the frigid sea.

In the 18th century, Spain claimed northern California. Its galleons sailed the coast and often wrecked there. Russian fur traders arrived in the early 19th century, establishing a colony and shipping otter pelts on a dangerous journey back to Russia. Spain and then Mexico governed until 1848 when the *Americanos* like John Fremont and Kit Carson arrived under a banner of Manifest Destiny.

The area had been busy with immigrants and supplies during the Gold Rush. Following statehood, the coast mostly returned to its roots, fishing and agriculture. A hundred years later, the windswept place at the edge of the Pacific looked much the same.

Bear rarely left Sonoma County. In fact, he had never been outside of Northern California. He figured, there wasn't much point. Still, there were signs he required a change, perhaps he was in need of more sunshine. He had learned about the Inca in grade school. It had made an impression. They worshipped the sun. That was a religion he could understand.

Bear felt a kinship with other sun-worshipers, like the heliotrope. His mother had grown them as annuals. Their flowers turned throughout the day to follow the sun. She had told him about the Greek words *helios* (sun) and *tropos* (to turn). That was the only Greek he knew.

He figured there was some *heliotropism* in his makeup as well. Fog made him cranky. It was *crazy-making* as his mother said. As a young boy, he'd worried about the heliotrope on a foggy day. How could it follow the sun, obscured by a thick mantle of fog? He'd even written a poem.

Sonoma Fog

It is damp and gray,
Like a grave stone in winter.
Steals the sun away,
Leaving us lost and bitter.
With no point of view,
The flower stares, without hope,
Into the dank brew,
The orphaned heliotrope.

Sometimes, the fog would linger all day. It was as if the earth had fallen out of orbit into a well of darkness.

Bear knew there were more demanding places. His father had told him about herding cattle in the Arizona desert and horses on a snowy Wyoming prairie. Yet, life on the coast was no picnic.

"I'll check over there," Curly said, as they rode up to Alvarez Creek.

"Let's split up," Bear suggested.

Bear Sargent was young, but already a skilled hand on horseback. He had been raised in a small house above Jenner by the Sea, which was little more than a store and a few homes on a hill. Jenner overlooked the mouth of the Russian River which emptied into the Pacific.

For the past year, Bear had been a ranch hand for the Bachman family. They owned 3,500 acres of grazing and timber land along the coast known as the Alvarez Creek Ranch. Henry Bachman was the family patriarch and ranch manager. His sons, Chet and Justin, had abandoned Sonoma for college on the east coast. Nobody thought they'd be coming back.

Suddenly, Bump was barking. Curly was up ahead staring into the creek bed. A barbed wire fence ran down the bank and across the creek to the other side. A sheep was tangled up in the wire. Splotches of red blood mixed in its wool. "That bugger's caught up in the fence. Shit!"

"How bad is it?" Bear asked, getting off the horse and walking over.

"Bad. I'll go back for some wire cutters," Curly said.

"Let me have a look," Bear replied. He slid down the creek bank. The sheep, a big ewe, reacted, getting more entangled in the fence, and bleating from the pain. Bear rested his arm on the sheep's back. "Whoa, there, girl," he said, soothingly. "We'll figure this out."

The ewe trembled. She was a hundred fifty pounds or more and strong. Bear didn't want to upset her more than necessary. Three strands of barbed wire were wrapped around her legs. "This won't be easy," he said, calmly.

He began unwinding the strands, taking his time, moving from front to back. Finally, the ewe came free. Holding her, he called up to Curly, "Throw me the hydrogen peroxide." Curly tossed him the bottle and Bear poured the liquid on the ewe's wounds.

"Don't forget your own scratches," Curly yelled at him.

Bear could see punctures on his hands and arms. His sleeves were in tatters. "That's it for this shirt," he said.

Bump found the other sheep a hundred feet distant, under a bay tree. They rode with the strays back to the rest of the flock a couple miles away. Bump did most the work, weaving back in forth, keeping the sheep in line. It reminded Bear of his first grade teacher, Mrs. Cruz, marching thirty kids to the cafeteria for their morning milk.

Bear was eighteen and away from home when his parents split up. His mom had returned to Nevada to care for an ailing relative and his father had moved to Oregon supposedly to fish. Bear's two older siblings had previously moved to San Diego and were waiting tables at a pizza place near San Diego State. His mom had later sent him a note. "You're a man now, and I know you can handle whatever happens. When in doubt, follow the sun."

He found work, shearing sheep. He had a talent for it. He had manned the sheep shearing booth at the Sonoma County Fair. He also had the equipment: harness which went around his waist to spare his back as he leaned over the sheep, the electric shears, even a generator since much of the shearing occurred in remote barns far from the grid.

He would go from ranch to ranch, charging by the head. The shearing season lasted only a couple months, in late spring after the lambs went to market.

Shearing day was a cacophony: a couple hundred sheep, baaing and bleating, the ranchers' whoops and h'yaws, and the rhythmic grind of the shears. It was important to move quickly and make clean cuts. The longer it took, the more agitated the sheep became.

The shears were kept sharp. If you nicked them, sheep would bleed. Bear had once jabbed the shears into the fleshy part of his palm. It bled like hell and left several v-shaped scars.

The shorn fleece was greasy with lanolin, grass, bugs and shit. You could get used to the smell, but it was strong. For those couple months, Bear carried that earthy odor. No bath or shower could wash it away.

The fleeces were gathered up, bound and thrown on a pile. The processors sent a truck to pick them up. From there, the wool was scoured, combed, sorted, dyed and spun. Bear abided this life. The shearing, herding, fencing and riding felt natural.

The fog rolled in and out. Days passed.

One night, the boss, Henry Bachman, asked Bear to sleep out with the sheep. It was spring and the coyotes had recently raided the flock seeking out young lambs. Bear had witnessed it before. It was gruesome to watch and worse to listen to, the high-pitched screams and the coyotes' gleeful cries.

Bear took a horse out to where the sheep were pastured. Bump came along. It was getting dark. Bear spread a tarp and sleeping bag.

He had a .30-06 and a 12 gauge. They were mostly for show. Without night vision, he wasn't going to be doing much shooting.

He had a headlamp, some paper and a pen. He could hear the flock around him. They would announce if coyotes were nearby. He tried writing about the moment.

Predator and Prey
A peaceful night,
In a long valley.
The sheep, aglow
In the moonlight,
Await death's tally.
Their canine foe
Attack on sight.
Take flight, run away.
The ancient rite,
Predator and prey.

Bear thought about editing his poem. Instead, he fed Bump and fell asleep. After midnight, Bear awoke to squeals and barking. The commotion was fifty feet to his right. He shined a flashlight over the area. Bump and three ewes were facing off against three coyotes.

Bear grabbed his shotgun and charged through the flock towards the disturbance, all the while yelling "Get outta here you sonsofbitches!" The coyotes did not retreat. He could see their open mouths and gnashing teeth. Bump was snarling and ready to pounce.

"Fuck this shit!" Bear yelled, and fired two shotgun blasts over the coyotes' heads. The noise sent all the animals scurrying. Bear ran after the coyotes, reloading and firing. One coyote dropped, wounded.

Bear continued in pursuit. He could hear Bump barking, coming up from behind. He turned towards Bump, trying to discourage the dog from chasing the two remaining coyotes. It was not necessary. The coyotes had already disappeared into the night.

Chet Bachman had graduated. He returned unexpectedly from Connecticut. His parents, Henry and Gloria Bachman, were overjoyed. "I'm not staying for long," Chet said, trying to dampen his parents' enthusiasm. "I have a proposition for Bear, if he's got some free time."

Curly was standing nearby and said, "I think he's up on the hill cleaning out the spring. I'll fetch him." The whole ranch received water from that spring. The water was collected, stored in a redwood tank then piped downhill.

Bear eventually walked into the house. He saw Henry and made a report. "The flow looks good at the spring. Just cleared the rocks out of the catch basin."

Chet came up and clapped him on the back. "Hey, Bear. What's going on, man?"

"Same old thing," Bear replied. The boys had been friends but not especially close. Chet was two years older and had no interest in the ranch business. They had spent a lot of time on horseback together when they were younger.

"Dad says things are kind of slow around here," Chet said. "I wondered if you might want to drive me back to the east coast, see the sights along the way. I'll pay."

"Why don't you just fly?" Bear asked.

"Well, thing is, I've got a classic BMW Z4, but it's not really running. It's parked at my old girlfriend's house in New Haven, Connecticut. I want to tow it back here and get it worked on."

Bear had a bare-bones GMC pick-up. It was ten years old and he wasn't sure it had the power to go six thousand miles, half of that towing another car.

"Please," Chet said, "think about it. Have you ever been out of the state?"

"Naw, never had much reason."

"Well, this is it. Time to see the world."

Gloria was watching the conversation. Bear thought he saw her roll her eyes. "How about some dinner boys?"

Bear and Chet set out the next day, heading east towards Reno. Bear drove, while Chet navigated. The GMC was a single cab with a bench seat and roll-down windows. The heater worked but there was no A/C. It was July so they decided to take I-80 and avoid some of the heat further south.

"Reno, Reno," Chet exclaimed, as they drove into town. "The Biggest Little City in the World!"

"Hey, I can read the sign," Bear replied, as they passed under the prominent sign, onto the city's main drag.

"Oooh!," Chet said, excitedly, "there's Harrah's. Let's play some blackjack."

They parked and walked into the casino. The temperature immediately dropped twenty degrees. Bear had never seen anything like it; bright lights, singing slots, high-waisted waitresses, stone-faced dealers and gonzo gamblers, all coexisting under a haze of cigarette smoke. Chet found a $1 blackjack table and bought them some chips.

Chet drank down a couple whiskeys. Bear nursed a beer. They managed to play for nearly an hour on ten bucks.

"I've smelled better after a day of shearing," Bear said, as they left the casino. They were back on the road, heading out of town.

To save money, they planned to camp as much as possible. They pulled off the highway outside Elko and camped near a dirt road. They'd done about five-hundred fifty miles that first day. Elko, at a mile high, cooled off nicely that night.

"I'm looking forward to showing you this country," Chet said, as they were waiting to fall asleep. "You know a lot about ranching, but I've seen the world. You won't believe New York City."

Bear used his hat to cover his eyes. "Maybe you can drive a little tomorrow. I'm beat." They slept well that night except for a few minutes when a couple coyotes came sniffing around their campsite.

Chet was a good tour guide. They hiked in the Snowy Mountains up in Wyoming and camped along the Platte River in Nebraska. The corn in Iowa was the best Bear had ever eaten. They took a boat tour on Lake Michigan while in Chicago and heard some music at a park in Cleveland. After a week, they arrived in New York City.

Chet had a roommate, Nathan, whose parents lived on 69th Street near Central Park West. They invited Chet and Bear to stay a few nights, while they explored the city. Bear felt too big for the space, especially with so many pieces of Asian statuary on display waiting to be toppled.

They walked to Battery Park, visited MOMA and toured Central Park. Bear's favorite spot, however, was the Meatpacking District. He liked talking to the butchers about their jobs, the cuts of meat, where the beef, pork and lamb came from. At the same time, they were fascinated by his stories of ranching out on the coast.

In the evenings, Chet, Bear and Nathan went to restaurants and music spots. One night, they had seen folk music at a mid-town bar. The songs had an anti-war theme. Bear hadn't thought much about the policy behind the War, but he did know people who were serving, some in Vietnam. So far he'd avoided the draft. Perhaps there wasn't much call for sheep farmers.

The three of them were walking through Times Square. It was late. The night was warm and humid. Chet and Nathan had been talking about a classmate. Suddenly, two men, medium build, one with a red bandana and the other with a John Deere hat, stepped out from an alley. Red bandana had a small caliber pistol and John Deere carried a broad-bladed hunting knife, which seemed excessive for the occasion. "Hold it, boys," Red bandana commanded.

Nathan had been trained in the ways of urban survival. "Don't hurt us," he said. Even without being asked, he was already reaching for his wallet. Chet was following suit, perhaps to divert attention from the fact that most of his money was in a pouch on his ankle and not in his wallet.

Bear stood still. Even without his hat, he was a few inches taller than the two strangers. More importantly, he was only a couple feet from Red bandana who was crowding in, trying too hard to be menacing. Bear had been around guns and knives his whole life, but he was not clear what this confrontation was about. For all he knew, these guys just wanted directions.

Red bandana gazed over at Nathan who was pulling his wallet from his pants. "Take it out slow," John Deere warned. That was all the evidence Bear needed. These guys were small time Jesse James and this was a stick up.

While the others were focused on Nathan, Bear reached over and took hold of Red bandana's right wrist and quickly wrenched it, along with the pistol, up and over the man's head. Bear then used his other hand to grab the pistol, which he now pointed at John Deere. "Drop the knife, friend." Adding the word "friend" made the request seem downright amiable. Bear made a show of checking that the safety was off and there was a round in the chamber. John Deere dropped the knife.

"We're leaving," Bear said, picking up the knife and gesturing for Chet and Nathan to move out. After a few blocks, Nathan said, "Holy shit, Bear. I can't believe you did that. That's not how most people react to being mugged."

"Sorry," Bear replied. "My first time."

A couple blocks from Nathan's building, Bear broke down and wiped off the pistol, discarding the clip, bullets and gun into different trashcans. He decided to keep the knife. It was good quality.

"Don't say anything to my parents," Nathan said. "They'd have a shit fit."

The next day, Chet and Bear drove up the Connecticut Turnpike to New Haven. Chet had graduated from Yale with a B.A. in Drama. He had ambitions of going to Yale's Drama School for a master's degree but had grown weary of academics. His new plan was to head to Hollywood, find an agent and lead a distinguished career as an actor.

Chet's former girlfriend, Lisa Goldstein, was studying to be a social worker at the University of New Haven. Lisa had been raised in New Haven, near the geographic feature known as West Rock, a prominent stone ridge. She had lost interest in Chet after he announced plans to move to Los Angeles. Lisa's family was firmly embedded in New Haven and she had zero interest in abandoning them.

There were no hard feelings. Lisa's family had agreed that Chet could leave his junker BMW in their driveway so long as he retrieved it within the month. They were happy to give Chet and Bear a place to stay for a night or two. Their main goal, as Lisa's parents said in private, was to *get that freaking heap of bolts outta here!*

Lisa's mother made them a nice dinner of chicken, potatoes and green beans. Everything was well cooked. Bear was grateful to have something other than lamb with mint sauce. The Goldsteins had a million questions for him about ranching and life in Sonoma. He was enjoying himself.

Chet, however, was sullen during the meal. He had confided on the drive from New York, that he still had feelings for Lisa but she had refused to even consider a move to L.A. For TV or film, you needed to go to L.A., New York or Vancouver.

Lisa was beautiful and smiled a lot. She exuded sympathy and Bear thought she'd make a wonderful social worker.

During dessert, a piece of carrot cake with maple icing, the door bell rang. A young man in his early twenties entered. He smiled at everyone. Lisa introduced him. "Chet and Bear, this is my friend Daryl Reisner, he's studying art at Albertus Magnus." Daryl looked like he'd been to the Summer of Love in San Francisco. He had wild curly hair and a shaggy goatee. He made the peace sign and said "Groovy".

Frankly, he looked like a lot of the folks who had come north from San Francisco into Marin, Sonoma and Mendocino counties, creating communes, practicing organic gardening, listening to the Dead and advancing the teachings of Baba Ram Dass.

Daryl said "Groovy" as Mrs. Goldstein explained that Bear lived near the coast in a redwood forest. Daryl's only complete sentence of the night concerned Andy Warhol's new exhibit called Raid the Icebox I at the Rhode Island School of Design. "He's taking stuff from the RISD's storage areas and curating it into a new exhibit. It's incredible. It's like redefining lost art."

Chet's response was perfect. "Wow, man."

After dinner, Bear and Chet were rinsing dishes. Bear leaned over and whispered, "You should stay here and save Lisa from that goofball."

Chet wasn't mature enough to see the wisdom in this suggestion. "Not groovy, man," he said, laughing. "I must pursue my acting. Besides, what does a Basque sheep herder know about these things. I don't see you with the perfect companion."

Bear continued rinsing, shaking his head. "Not groovy, man! Not groovy at all!"

Attaching Chet's beater BMW to the GMC's trailer hitch was nearly impossible. They had bought a triangular harness from a local U-Haul that allowed them to hook the BMW's front bumper to the tow hitch. But first, two of the BMW's tires were flat and had to be patched. After two days, they were ready to start the trip back to California.

The Goldsteins were gracious with their goodbyes. Bear gave Lisa a big hug, whispering that Chet was a fool not to stay.

Lisa laughed and shrugged. "His loss."

The Goldsteins cheered as the GMC pulled out of the driveway towing the BMW scrapheap. Chet was quiet. A lot of guys are like that when they've forfeited their one chance at true happiness. But, as Bear had learned from several people he'd met in New Haven, *whatcha gonna do?* There was the open road ahead and, despite the uncertainty of things, Bear felt good about it.

The trip was uneventful until St. Louis. It was a Sunday afternoon. They had crossed the Mississippi on Interstate 70 when the BMW's bumper came loose on one side. "Shit!" Bear said, "the car's unhitched. Look back there. Tell me what you see."

Chet turned around and looked. "It looks like the bumper is only attached to the right side of the BMW's frame." As a result, the BMW was swerving like a junker possessed. "Better stop or it's going to come loose altogether." It wasn't a pleasant thought leaving the BMW in a lane of traffic. Somebody was sure to hit it.

Bear slowed immediately and edged cautiously to the far right lane. He took the first exit, a near empty downhill ramp. It deposited them in an industrial zone of warehouses and factories. It was Sunday. Nothing seemed to be open. "There!" Chet yelled, pointing. A modest looking eatery called Red's Café, was sandwiched between Jimmy's Welding and Archway Trucking. The café was open. Its parking lot was empty except for two cars. Bear pulled in and parked as best he could.

There was a neon *Open* sign in the window. They walked in. It must have been a hundred degrees outdoors but, inside Red's, it was cool and the lights were low. A TV on the wall was carrying a baseball game between the Cardinals and the Dodgers. Chet started yammering a mile a minute. "Our tow hitch came loose and we're swerving all over the place and we're trying to tow the damn car back to California but we'll never make it at this rate."

The proprietor, whom they assumed was Red, was staring at Chet. The only customer did not even turn around, but just kept on watching the ball game.

Bear tried a different tack. "Hi, I'm Bear Sargent. I wonder if there's any chance of finding Jimmy who owns the welding shop. I think with some iron, a torch and a drill I could fix the problem. We're happy to pay whatever it costs."

The mention of money seemed to arouse the customer's interest. "I'm Jimmy. This game's almost over. Then we'll talk."

Bear ordered a burger and a beer. Chet had the fish and chips and started chanting "Beat LA, Beat LA" as if he was at Candlestick Park.

Jimmy led them to his shop next door. It was a functional shop with all the equipment one might need for any welding job. Bear had experience with welding and he and Jimmy collaborated designing a fix.

They were both practical. They decided the old bumper had to go. It was too flimsy and, besides, would be tough to re-attach to the chassis. Jimmy found a length of four inch angle iron which they bolted to the BMW's frame. The angle iron would serve as a rather stout substitute for the old chrome bumper.

They then drilled two holes in the angle iron and bolted the trailer hitch directly into it. It was, from an engineering point of view, a thing of great simplicity and, therefore, great beauty.

Chet paid Jimmy his price and, at Bear's urging, fifty bucks more. They shared a beer then said goodbye to Jimmy. Amazingly, they were back on the road before nightfall.

"Goddamn, Chet. That was nothing short of a miracle," Bear said, after they'd been driving for a while. "I'm mean, it's Sunday, in the factory district. We find an open restaurant whose only customer owns a welding shop and who just happens to have the materials and equipment to fix the problem."

"Well, we paid for it," Chet said.

"So what? It was a miracle. I'll never complain again." Bear was resolving to be a happy heliotrope and keep his face turning towards the sun. He jabbed Chet in the shoulder for emphasis.

"Whatever," Chet replied. He wasn't comprehending the significance of the moment. "I've got bigger issues. Like, what am I going to do? Can I make it as an actor? Can I pretend to be someone I'm not?"

"You've done a pretty good job so far," Bear kidded.

Chet ignored the barb. "Will I regret not staying in New Haven? And if Lisa ends up with that Daryl prick, I may have to shoot myself."

"Couldn't you be happy doing something other than acting?" Bear asked. "I mean, is there really a perfect job?" Maybe, he thought, it was enough to find something that gave you a sense of purpose and, of course, some income. "I enjoyed building that bumper with Jimmy back there. We did something together and shared a beer and it served a purpose. All I'm saying is, you don't have to be a movie star. There are lots of roles to play."

Chet seemed to be thinking about it. "Maybe it was Yale. People there are always talking about what they're going to do next. The present is just a stepping stone. Like, 'I better take that economics class so I can go to Harvard Business School' or 'I need to know Latin and Greek if I want to teach the Classics' or 'I need organic chemistry to be a doctor' or 'I better marry an extrovert if I'm going into politics'. It's like a *success death loop*. Since I studied I drama, I better show them I can be a good actor."

"Yeah, heaven forbid, you run a sheep ranch or sell insurance," Bear said.

"Easy for you to say, *world's best sheep shearer*!" Chet said, with a laugh.

They continued west on Interstate 70. Two days later they were in western Colorado. They climbed slowly to nearly 11,000 feet to Vail Summit and took the exit to the Vail Ski Resort. There, they rode Gondola #1 to Vail Mountain and hiked for a while.

"I think that's the Continental Divide over there," Chet said, pointing to a tall range just miles away.

"Oh, yeah?" Bear said, not really sure what that meant. "What is it exactly?"

"Uh, it divides the country into two watersheds. To the west, rivers and streams run to the Pacific and, to the east, water heads towards the Atlantic."

Bear had heard his mom refer to a *watershed* moment which was supposedly a big deal. "So," Bear said, I guess a 'watershed moment' would mean a major change, like when things change direction."

"Sure, or maybe it means you're all wet," Chet said, chuckling at his own joke.

It was a sunny day with incredible views. They decided to hike back down the mountain to the village. They had some pizza and were back on the road. They drove for a few more hours then found a place to camp. They cooked up some beef stroganoff on the camp stove and had a cup of hot cocoa before sacking out. It was a cool night. An owl was hooting in the woods. It was dark and quiet.

"You know," Bear said, staring skyward from his sleeping bag, "this trip has been kind of a watershed moment for me. I've learned some stuff, good stuff."

"Me too," Chet agreed. "For one, I'm happy just being here."

There was a dance the following weekend in Monte Rio, a few miles up the Russian River. It was held in the Monte Rio Theater, a corrugated steel Quonset hut which had been purchased as salvage from the Navy in 1949. The design had been named after the Navy base at Quonset Point, Rhode Island where the huts were first used.

Bear and Chet had goaded each other into going. Neither of them was much of a dancer. "I bet there'll be girls there," Chet said. His argument had carried the day.

The theater was packed. Chet and Bear saw a couple women their age sitting near the dance floor. It was too noisy, with the music and conversations, to hear anything.

"Would you girls like to dance?" Bear asked in a loud voice.

The women looked at each other, shrugged and stood up. The taller one extended a hand to Bear. "Let's go," she said. "I'm Jessie. My friend is Cecilia." After the introductions, they walked to the dance floor. Bear's moves resembled Godzilla taking a stroll in Tokyo.

Later, after several dances, the four of them were sitting at a table. Cecilia asked Chet what he planned to do now that he was out of college.

Chet thought about it. "Well," he said, "being here with you is a pretty good start."

Bear laughed. "Who says college boys can't learn?"

The band came back from a break and began a new song. "I like these guys," Jessie said. "But not the easiest music to dance to."

"And the songs are so long," Cecilia agreed.

After the song ended, the bearded leader of the band made an announcement. "Hey, for anybody who's on the east coast, we'll be playing up in Bethel, New York next month. It's an outdoor thing at a place called Yasgur's farm. Hey man, everybody'll be there."

"Wanna go?" Chet asked.

Bear was nodding as a Beatles lyric was playing in his head:

One day, you'll find, that I have gone,
But tomorrow may rain, so
I'll follow the sun.
Yes, tomorrow may rain, so
I'll follow the sun.

HABITAT

James W. Poindexter

Bobby Epstein, at 14, was the youngest of the three Epstein boys. He slouched in his dad's easy chair, consuming an after-school snack of Fritos and orange Fanta, while watching the big-screen TV that covered one wall of the family room.

Normally, Bobby would have been playing his favorite video game, *Crop Dusters*. The game was addictive in the way any carrot and stick, punishment and reward activity can be. The goal of the game was to spray *PESTicide* (a special mixture of DDT and plutonium) from a biplane onto your enemies without damaging nearby crops, citizens or property. Players were rated based on technique and accuracy and there were severe penalties for spraying anything other than pests, ghouls and zombies.

Today, however, Bobby was watching a new TV series called *Detention*. The series was an updated version of the Molly Ringwald movie, *The Breakfast Club*. A diverse group of teens meet in after-school detention and together plot the overthrow of student government. Despite the antics and canned laughter, Bobby was not into it. He was having trouble shaking the after-school fatigue. He couldn't even muster the energy to get up from the chair, although he felt some urgency to go to the bathroom.

The TV show paused for a commercial break. "Are you between the ages of fourteen and sixteen?" the announcer asked in an upbeat voice. Bobby had not seen the ad before. The message seemed to be directed right at him, which was odd.

Bobby wasn't usually the target of any ads other than for sugary drinks and cereals. His group, early teens, had no money or power. The early teen years kind of *sucked*. There was little pride, no self-respect. His mom had said, "Beggars can't be choosers." Well, he was fed up. He wanted some control. He was sick of groveling and constantly being told to *keep his nose clean,* whatever that meant.

The announcer was a chill looking guy, maybe nineteen or twenty, bearded with longish hair. His sincere face filled the TV. He had a calm way of talking. "How many of you are aware of the new law passed by Congress called the *Teen Emancipation Act* or TEA? Well, wake up and smoke the TEA!" the man said with a jovial laugh. "That law gives you the right to opt out of school and join *HABITAT*."

Bobby was about to graduate from middle school and had recently asked his father if he could defer going to high school. "I'd rather shovel shit at a pig farm," Bobby had said, never having seen a pig farm. His father had conveniently failed to mention the *Teen Emancipation Act.*

"Look," the announcer continued, "HABITAT is a national service program, with major funding through the Department of Health and Human Services. It places you for one year with other teens in a rural area or central city. You work together to build housing for the housing disadvantaged, whom we call inHABITATants."

Bobby wanted to be taken seriously, but he knew from first hand experience that teenagers got no respect. They were pawns. Their only job was to *meet expectations* and *don't piss me off.* Bobby's last report card had noted, "Seems bored, mind wanders, could do better." It wasn't his fault school was so lame.

The ad showed teens at work building tiny homes, while the announcer said, "Don't let the adults in your life tell you otherwise. You have the absolute right to leave school and join *HABITAT*. This program is not for everyone. You need to be a self-starter, somebody who wants to contribute to society."

Bobby had always wanted to be part of something. Other organizations, like the Army or Americorps, required you to be eighteen. He didn't want to wait!

"And," the spokesman continued, "what's best of all, we will pay for your travel, food and housing. If you're interested, call us. There's no obligation. Opportunities await!"

A phone number was now flashing on the screen along with the command, *Call now, Call now, Call now!* Bobby needed to talk to someone, but his parents were at work and his older brothers were busy with after-school sports. As usual, he was alone and *bored out of his gourd*. Bobby had heard enough. He called the number.

* * *

That evening, all hell broke loose. It started at dinner, the usual conversation. His brothers talked about sports and an upcoming dance. His father and mother shared some gossip from work. But mostly, they peppered Bobby with questions about his classes, friends and activities.

“What about you Bobby?” his dad asked. “What’s new?”

“Not much. Came home. Watched TV. Waited for you guys,” Bobby said, summing up his afternoon.

“Sounds kind of dull, Bobby,” his mom said. “Don’t you have some homework you could do when we’re not here?”

“I suppose,” Bobby said, deciding what to say next. “I learned something new today, about the Teen Emancipation Act.”

His parents and brothers gasped. They ceased eating and stared at him. “Terrible law!” his father exclaimed. “Destroys parental authority.”

Bobby felt intimidated but soldiered on. “I’ve thought about it,” he said. “My age group, fourteen to sixteen, we feel worthless. Nobody wants anything from us other than a positive attitude and good grades. I need to do something that’s meaningful.”

“Well, you could come to my office and do some filing,” his mom offered.

“Yeah,” his dad agreed, "and there’s always taking out the trash and cutting back the blackberry bush.”

His brothers were less helpful. One called him “a little prick.” The other added, mockingly, “Hi, I’m Bobby. I’m special!”

One of Bobby’s teachers had told him that fourteen year olds had once participated in society, such as hunting, farming, weaving, cooking, making things, going to market, basically a host of useful tasks. It was only in the past hundred years or so, they’d been locked away in schools and denied any meaningful role. Nowadays, they were viewed as an annoyance, possibly useful one day but, for the present, little more than a lump of clay.

Bobby refused to sit there, taking insults from a family whom he loved but who were clearly oblivious to his needs. “Look,” he said, “I’ve already signed up. They’re sending me to San Francisco to build tiny houses for HABITAT.”

“What?” his mother said, gawking at him.

“I’m leaving right after graduation,” Bobby said, defiantly.

* * *

The Greyhound Bus slowed for traffic on the upper deck of the Bay Bridge. Bobby stared out the window. This was his first trip alone and his first time in San Francisco. It was all new. HABITAT had given him few instructions, other than when and where to catch the bus.

His seat-mate, an older woman, probably in her thirties, had befriended him on the trip. She was pointing out the sites. “Over there is Alcatraz. And there’s a ferry and, up there, that’s Coit Tower above Telegraph Hill. Oh, and here comes the Ferry Building. See the clock tower?” Bobby was definitely not a city boy. He had spent his whole life in Winters, a town of about ten thousand in rural Yolo County. He had crossed smaller bridges over the Sacramento River, but these bridges were miles long. The Bay was enormous.

It was late afternoon. The driver took a downtown exit and pulled into the main bus station at Mission and First streets. The HABITAT office was a mile away at the corner of Ninth and Mission. A mile did not sound too far, so he decided to walk.

Bobby felt dwarfed by the crowds and skyscrapers outside the terminal. He set off up Mission Street, pulling his suitcase behind him. The architecture changed suddenly from modern glass and steel to older timber and brick buildings. The streets, structures and people seemed shabbier.

The HABITAT office was on the ground floor of the Spotter Hotel. The hotel advertised *Monthly and Hourly Rates*. The sign over the office door said ***HABITAT for Those in Need.*** Bobby walked up a couple steps to the entry and tried the door. It was locked. He couldn't find a bell so he knocked. "Hello? Anybody there?"

A man in his forties, with a graying beard and wispy hair tied back in a ponytail, opened the door, smiling, revealing pointy and slightly yellowed teeth. "You must be Bobby Epstein," he said, pleasantly, "Come in."

Bobby stepped in, somewhat reluctantly. "Hello. Yes, I'm Bobby."

The man ushered him in. "Welcome, Bobby. I'm Bongo Badger. I'm the local HABITAT manager." He led Bobby to a small conference room and pointed to a chair. "Have a seat. Here's a copy of the brochure for you to read. Then, we can talk about your assignment."

Bobby browsed the brochure, too excited to concentrate. "Where will I be staying?" he asked.

"Oh, upstairs with the rest of the volunteers. I'll show you after we go over a few things."

There was something disquieting about Mr. Badger. His face was bony, almost skull-like; however, he wore nice clothes, a button down shirt with cuff links, khakis and leather shoes. Apart from his preppy clothes, Badger resembled the Crypt Keeper from the old TV series.

Bobby was shown to his room on the third floor. Another boy was already there lying on one of the twin beds. "Bobby, this is your roommate, JJ Rabbit." JJ was fifteen. He had dropped out of high school back in Boise and signed up for HABITAT. JJ was a beefy kid, who had spent much of his free time playing video games. He and Bobby had much in common. Both were eager to move on.

After dinner that night, Badger knocked on their door and walked in. "Hey boys, tomorrow we'll be going to our Turk Street project up in the Tenderloin. We're building thirty new tiny houses on a vacant lot. You'll start off as lumpers. Make yourselves useful. Haul stuff when asked. And most of all, observe how things are done."

"When can we start building things ourselves?" Bobby asked.

"Soon enough. Just get the hang of it for now," Badger answered. "Half of the units are already built and occupied. Never disturb the residents. This is their home. They like their privacy." Badger eyed them intently, driving home the point. "Anyway, there are fifteen units to go. We move qualified homeless people into the new units as they are built." He paused. "One more thing," he continued, "I'll need your cell phones. We'll give the phones back on Sundays so you can call home."

The "No Devices" rule had been emphasized in the application package. The boys weren't happy about it, but handed their phones over to Badger. They noticed there were no TVs or even radios in the room.

"What do we do in our free time?" Bobby asked.

"Read, talk, play checkers," Badger suggested. Neither boy had ever been without electronics. *Reality* was not something they were accustomed to. It was weird.

"How many volunteers are there?" JJ asked.

"Fourteen of you, all have rooms in this building."

"And how many supervisors?" Bobby asked.

"Well, I'm in charge of the volunteers and also finding new residents, the *inHABITATants,* for the tiny homes. You'll meet Debra Byrne tomorrow. She oversees the construction work. Anything else?"

"Where's the bathroom?" Bobby asked, suddenly needing to pee.

"End of the hall," Badger said, pointing. "And, for your safety, each floor is locked down at night. There's an emergency exit out to the fire escape, but otherwise nobody goes out at night. This isn't the safest neighborhood. Okay?"

"Got it," the boys responded.

"Alright. We'll serve breakfast at 6:30. Everybody volunteers in the kitchen. You'll get a KP schedule tomorrow."

After Badger left, Bobby asked, "What's KP?"

"My grandpa was in Vietnam," JJ said. "I think it means *kitchen police* or *kitchen patrol*, but my grandpa used to joke that it just meant *keep peeling* 'cause they had to peel so many vegetables."

Bobby had trouble sleeping the first night. The room itself was okay, but the street lights shone through the windows and the traffic noise continued all night. The worst moment was at two a.m. Bobby had to go to the bathroom, but was reluctant to venture out into the hallway. He eventually mustered the courage and opened the door. The lighting in the hall was dim and creepy. The carpet felt stiff on his bare feet, as if it hadn't been cleaned. The bathroom at the end of the hall had one exposed twenty watt bulb, which cast ominous shadows

When Bobby returned to the room, JJ was awake. "Everything okay?" he whispered.

"Went down the hall to the bathroom," Bobby explained. "It's creepy out there."

"Lock the door," JJ said.

Bobby fumbled around the door handle. "I don't see a lock." He lifted a small chair and stuck it in front of the door.

"I don't think that'll keep the boogey man out," JJ said, giggling.

Bobby found the laughter reassuring. He fell into bed and was soon asleep.

* * *

Bobby had been at HABITAT for two weeks. He felt happy. He was learning new things and working with other kids who were becoming his friends. He was no longer a lumper, having graduated to assistant framer. His new job was to cut and secure the joists, studs and rafters, basically the tiny house's skeleton.

He enjoyed working outdoors, sometimes in sun, sometimes in fog. The San Francisco weather defied the usual rules of summertime. Up in his town of Winters, summer temps were often over a hundred. He preferred the cool Bay air. Overall, he was happy to be free of the cramped desks and strictures of school.

HABITAT's Turk Street site was nearly half a city block. It was cordoned off by a construction fence. The project's entrance was a chainlink gate. Next to the gate, a large sign said: **A HABITAT Project, Department of Health and Human Services**.

The site had been graded and graveled. Half of the planned houses had already been built, each to the same specifications. Each house was ten by fifteen feet with a pitched roof and a small front porch. The plan included a barebones kitchen, bathroom and sitting area on the main floor and a loft for sleeping. The house exteriors were painted different colors, emphasizing a Mexican color scheme of oranges, yellows, greens and blues.

The volunteers were mostly boys and a few girls. They had been sorted into teams. Bobby's team included his roommate JJ, two other boys, Tony and Jesse, and a girl, Tessa. Tessa was the most knowledgeable when it came to building things. Her father was a contractor. Unlike the rest of them, who had to beg their parents to let them go, Tessa's father had been the one to urge her to join HABITAT, telling her to *take a year off and learn something useful.*

* * *

One morning, Bobby and Tessa were in the kitchen at the hotel, making sandwiches for the crew's lunch. "You miss your family at all?" Tessa asked, while spreading mustard on multiple slices of bread.

"Not really," Bobby said. "I talk to them on Sundays during family time. Once a week seems about right. Back home, I was starting to feel like a punching bag."

Badger stuck his head through the kitchen door. "Hurry it up, we're due at the job site."

They quickly added the ham and cheese and lettuce, wrapped the sandwiches, and inserted them with some chips and a cookie into brown paper bags. On their way out to join the others, Tessa asked, "Have you met any of the inHABITATants yet? There's a guy named Oliver in unit three. He's kind of a character."

"Not yet, but I'd like to," Bobby said, struggling with the lunch bags he was balancing in his hands.

The morning shift did not go smoothly.

An OSHA inspector assigned to the project made a surprise visit. Her name was Toots McShea and she took her job seriously. OSHA was responsible for assuring the workplace complied with strict child labor safety standards. The Teen Emancipation Act had promised to keep volunteers safe from harm.

During the inspection, Ms. McShea asked the volunteers if they had any complaints about conditions on the job site. They all said things were alright. Ms. McShea handed a card to Bobby. "If you ever need any help, give me a call."

The inspection angered their supervisor, Debra Byrne. They had lost valuable time. Debra yelled, "Get back to work!"

Also that morning, Bobby cut a piece of siding an inch too short. Debra, still steaming, chewed him out. "Dammit, Bobby. I keep telling you, *measure twice, cut once*. We can't waste lumber." Bobby knew he had no defense. He had been talking to somebody when he screwed up the measurement.

Despite these glitches, the team had that day finished the latest tiny house. There were now seventeen completed structures. Bobby was impressed. The latest unit was sturdy and plumb and had been approved for human habitation.

Back in school, Bobby's only source of pride had been an occasional good grade. There wasn't much else to gloat about. Seeing the finished tiny house, however, gave him a sense of accomplishment. He was happy to be a part of the team.

Supervisor Debra marked the occasion with a short speech. "You should be proud of yourselves. Life's not just about finding a way to earn money. It's important to do things that are useful. Things you can look at and appreciate. And, if you do things as a team, so much the better. So keep up the good work!" The kids hooted and hollered.

Debra took a group photo that day. Bobby and Tessa were standing in front, holding their hammers high above their heads. "I'll send you copies," Debra promised.

During the afternoon break, Tessa led Bobby over to Tiny House #3. There was a man sitting on a chair on the minuscule front porch. "Hi there, Oliver," Tessa said. "This is my friend Bobby."

The man looked old. He wore glasses and was super thin. He had little hair and a wrinkled face. "Good to meet you, sir," Bobby said, politely. "If you don't mind my asking, where were you before here?" It wasn't clear where the residents came from.

"That's a long story," Oliver confided. "I ended up on the streets, in a tent over on Eddy Street. I heard about this place and applied. My social worker helped."

"How'd you end up in a tent?" Bobby added. He'd never met anyone who was homeless.

"Typical story," Oliver said. He explained that it had started with an illness, a hospital visit and no insurance. Debts piled up and he had no job. His wife and daughter left to live with her parents. He developed an addiction to pain meds, followed by stints in rehab, all of which worsened his financial woes. Currently, he was sober and living off a small disability income.

"There must be a lot of people wanting to get in here," Tessa said.

"Oh yeah. But nothin's for free. They expect you to work, that's for sure," Oliver replied, vaguely.

Bobby wanted to know what work Oliver was doing, but before he could ask the question, they could hear Badger a ways away calling for them. They said goodbye to Oliver and ran to where Badger was standing. "What's up, boss?" Tessa rasped, short of breath.

Badger wagged his finger. "Don't talk to the residents. They're entitled to some privacy."

Bobby was curious about what the residents did every day. Oliver had said HABITAT expected him to work. Bobby had sometimes noticed that Oliver and other residents went out during the day. That was surprising since Bobby had been told that being homeless *and* unemployed were criteria for living at HABITAT.

He brought it up one day at lunch with his team, Tessa, JJ, Tony and Jesse. "You see those guys leaving every morning?" Bobby ask.

"Yeah," Jesse said, "Where do they go?"

"I'm going to find out," Bobby said.

* * *

The next morning, Bobby got his chance. Supervisor Debra needed some screws and staples from the local hardware store. He had run errands before and was familiar with the neighborhood. He noticed that several of the inHABITATants, including Oliver, were conversing with Badger near the project entrance. Their meeting ended and the residents walked out onto the street.

Bobby followed.

Badger called to him, "Where you going?"

"Debra wants some things at the hardware store."

"Well, get it done quick."

Bobby walked through the gate, trailing behind one group of residents The group headed in roughly the same direction as the hardware store. They walked down to Market then left on Powell Street, a few blocks to the entrance of the St. Francis Hotel on Union Square. Bobby watched as the men broke up into pairs, spreading out around the square.

Oliver and his partner stood near the St. Francis steps. Hotel guests and tourists scurried back and forth. Oliver's partner started talking loudly. He sounded like a huckster at a carnival. He wore a big smile and had an engaging voice. He told stories of haunted rooms in the hotel and nefarious crimes on the square. The crowd compressed, some listening intently, while others tried to walk around.

Bobby recognized what they were doing. It was a classic *sandwich* technique. He had seen it demonstrated in a PBS documentary about street crime in Barcelona. Oliver's partner was the *stall,* while Oliver was the *pick.* Oliver pretended to be jostled, while reaching into purses, pockets and bags for wallets, jewelry and phones. It was easy pickings, like fishing in a trout pond. In fifteen minutes, they had caught their limit and moved on to another part of the square.

Bobby ran to the hardware store. He didn't want to be tardy returning to work. At lunch, he reported to his friends what he had seen.

"You think the guys living here are pickpockets?" Tessa asked.

"I'm just saying what I saw," Bobby said.

"These are street people," JJ said. "Where would they learn those kinds of skills?"

Nobody knew the answer. They agreed not to mention it to anyone until they had a better grasp of what was going on.

* * *

The next morning, Badger announced at breakfast that they would have a visitor. "Daniel Chickens, the CEO of HABITAT, will be visiting us today at the job site. There will also be some people from the press. Work hard and only speak if someone asks you a question. Just say you enjoy working here, helping the community. That sort of thing. Any questions?"

Bobby wanted to ask why some of the inHABITATants appeared to be involved in a pickpocket ring, but decided this was not the right time. Instead, he asked, "How many projects like this does HABITAT have? And why's he coming to this one?"

"There are about two hundred projects nationwide and all of them have government backing. He usually checks in with us when he's in California."

Construction continued until the mid-afternoon break. The volunteers and visitors gathered by some picnic tables set up for the occasion. Bobby saw Debra standing near the project gate, talking to Badger and a gray haired man along with some press people. The group walked over to where the volunteers were seated.

"Guys," Badger announced, "this is Mr. Chickens. He's our boss from HABITAT's headquarters in New York."

There was sporadic applause as the CEO stepped forward. "Good to see you all out here. You're doing a fine job, a fine job!" He said, nodding at the group. "I realize you don't get much money." Several people laughed. "But, if it wasn't for volunteers like you, these houses would never be built and the residents here would have no place to live. They'd be back on the streets. So, between your labor and the government's generous investment, we're able to provide these people with a clean and safe home."

Bobby thought Chickens' speech was inspiring. It was true that they only received room and board and a little pocket money. They were, however, doing something useful. That felt like ample compensation.

Tessa looked at Bobby and whispered, "Wonder where all the residents are? You'd think they'd be here to thank Chickens in person."

"Maybe they're out hustling again," Bobby said. "I have to run an errand after break. I'll check it out."

Bobby was sent to the hardware store. He detoured to Union Square and again spotted Oliver and his partner on the Macy's side of Union Square. As before, they were running a pickpocket ruse on unsuspecting tourists. This time Oliver was performing magic tricks with playing cards. As the crowd gathered, his partner was doing the bump and grab.

Bobby watched for a while, then walked quickly to the hardware store.

By the time Bobby returned to the work site, he could see the crews putting away their tools and closing up for the day. On the other side of the site, where the houses had already been built, he could see Oliver and several other men gathering in front of one of the empty houses that had recently been completed. Badger was on the unit's front porch gesturing for one of the men to enter. After the first man had entered and left, the next man entered.

Bobby walked over to supervisor Debra and handed her the supplies he had brought from the hardware store.

“You took long enough,” she said.

“I made a wrong turn,” he apologized.

Bobby spotted his friends hovering at the break table. They often hung out there at the end of the day waiting for the van to take them back to the hotel. He told them what he had seen.

“What do you think Badger was doing?” Tessa asked.

“Maybe he’s the guy who fences the stuff the guys bring in,” Bobby speculated.

“We need a plan,” JJ said.

“Yeah,” Tony and Jesse agreed.

The problem was they needed evidence. A kid couldn’t suspect a crime had occurred and expect it to stick. However, their phones were kept in a box in Badger’s bedroom, except for a few hours each Sunday. They would need at least one phone to document what was going on. Tessa interrupted, “Okay, here’s the plan.”

That night, after ten, an alarm sounded on the hotel’s fourth floor. Badger, awakened by the alarm, ran up the stairs from his room, unlocking the main door to each floor as he climbed. On the fourth floor, he found the emergency exit open at the end of the hallway. Tessa was on the landing smoking a cigarette. “Sorry,” she said, nonchalantly, “I needed some air.”

Badger was furious. “Hell no! Never open these doors!” he shouted. “And goddamn it! No smoking!”

While Badger was thus engaged, Bobby ran from his room down the stairs to the second floor and Badger's room. He found the box containing the volunteers' cell phones. He rustled around in the box until he found his own phone, then ran back up the stairs.

JJ was waiting for him on the third floor. They were standing by their bedroom door when Badger came storming down from the fourth floor. "False alarm. Go back to bed," he said, locking the third floor door and heading downstairs to his own room.

* * *

The next morning, Badger hurried the crew off to work with only a carton of juice and a breakfast bar. Tessa hadn't shown up. Somebody asked where she was. Badger was still angry. All he said was, "She's being punished for her bad behavior last night."

The crew went through the motions. Bobby was worried about Tessa. At lunch with JJ, Tony and Jesse, he brought it up. "Why isn't she here?"

"Maybe," Tony said, "Badger confined her to her room."

"I'm worried about her," Bobby said. He patted his jacket pocket, feeling for his phone. "Whatever we're going to do, we better do it soon."

"We better get some evidence or forget it." Jesse added.

"Maybe check out the empty house where you saw Badger taking stuff from Oliver and the other guys" JJ said. "You could use your phone to take some photos."

"Good idea," Bobby agreed. "But then what? We need to get some adult involved."

The group thought that was a good idea but couldn't decide whether to call the police or maybe involve their supervisor Debra Byrne or the CEO Daniel Chickens. "Can we trust any of the HABITAT people?" Bobby asked.

"Good point," replied JJ. "How about the OSHA inspector, Toots McShea? She's not part of HABITAT and she's supposed to look out for our safety."

"Yeah," Bobby said, "and she left me her card so I have her number. But first, I need to get into that house where I saw Badger."

Bobby waited until late in the day before he had an opportunity. He asked to be excused to use the bathroom, which consisted of three Honey Bucket commodes and an outdoor wash basin. He hid behind the porta-potties and, from there, ran down the row of completed houses to the one where he had previously seen Badger and the residents.

Once there, Bobby snuck around to the side window and peered in. He couldn't believe what he saw. Tessa was sitting on the floor, tied up and gagged. He knocked softly on the window. She stared up at him, looking frightened. He could also see shelves and boxes, presumably full of stolen goods.

He tried to lift the window, but it was locked. He had anticipated as much. He pulled duct tape from his pocket and taped one the window panes. He then pulled a hammer from his tool belt and gently pounded the pane until it cracked and the glass fell free. He put his hand through the opening and unlatched the window. Once the window was open, he hoisted himself up and through into the room. He quickly untied Tessa.

“We have to get out of here!” Tessa urged. “They’re coming back soon.”

Bobby had taken a photo of Tessa tied up. He was now making a video of the wallets, keys, watches and jewelry that he found in the various boxes around the room. There was a lot of loot. He then made a call to Toots McShea at OSHA. The call went into voice mail.

“Ms. McShea, it’s Bobby Epstein at the HABITAT project. We have evidence that some of the residents are running a pickpocket ring and our supervisor Bongo Badger is the leader, fencing the stolen goods. They kidnapped one of the volunteers, Tessa. She’s with me now. I’m texting you photos and a video of the stuff.”

Just then, they heard voices approaching the front door. “Let’s get out of here!” Tessa whispered.

They crept through the open window and cowered at the side of the building, as the men were stepping onto the front porch. Badger’s voice was clear. “We’ll get her out of here tonight when it’s dark.”

Bobby pointed to the back of the house. “Stay low,” he said softly.

Badger’s group entered the house. One of them called out, “She’s gone!” Another said, “They’re in back of the house!”

Tessa said, “Run!” Bobby dropped his tool belt and took off towards the front gate. Tessa was next to him. He noticed she was still in her pajamas and barefoot. There was something incongruous about seeing her in panda bear pajamas being pursued by a gang of thieves.

Four men, including Badger, were getting closer. The guard at the gate seemed unsure what to do. “Let us out!” Bobby yelled. “Medical emergency!” He held his wrist as if he had suffered some grievous injury. The guard opened the gate and they rushed through.

They ran east on Turk Street through the Tenderloin towards Market Street. They crossed Turk against oncoming cars and buses. They dodged a homeless encampment of tents and grocery carts. Bobby could see their pursuers getting closer.

Bobby's phone rang. It was Toots McShea. "Where are you Bobby?" she asked.

"We're running on Turk near Market. Four men including Bongo Badger are after us on foot."

"I've called the police. Take Market to Powell and go into the St. Francis Hotel to the reception desk. Can you do that?"

"We'll try," Bobby said. "C'mon," he urged Tessa, "Let's get to the St. Francis."

They reached Market. The men were fifty feet behind, dodging crowds and street vendors. After turning left onto Powell, by the cable car turnaround, Bobby and Tessa continued up the hill. By the time they reached the St. Francis steps, Badger's gang was only twenty feet behind.

"Keep going," Bobby urged, as they ran up the stairs. The uniformed doorman saw them coming and opened the heavy glass door as they charged through.

Badger was obviously desperate. He couldn't allow Bobby or Tessa to talk. He led his men into the hotel.

Inside, the hubbub of the streets was gone. It was replaced by high ceilings, plush carpet, muted voices and a string quartet playing Mozart.

Bobby and Tessa spotted the reception desk. Badger's group was now only feet away and about to pounce when a loud voice called out, "Police, stop! Step away from those kids!"

* * *

Later that day, the authorities descended on the project site. There was Lieutenant Thomas from SFPD, Toots McShea from OSHA, even Daniel Chickens from HABITAT. The stolen goods had been recovered and the crimes by Badger and his ring had been revealed.

Lieutenant Thomas summed it up. "Bongo Badger was responsible for placing new residents in the tiny houses. However, he offered preferences to residents who were willing to join the pickpocket ring. As it turns out, he had a record and passed his skills as a pickpocket onto them. He also threatened to evict any residents who blew the whistle on the operation."

"What about the kidnapping?" Bobby asked. "Why did they tie up Tessa?"

Thomas shrugged, "Badger became suspicious after the hotel alarm went off last night. He noticed one of your phones was missing. He confronted Tessa but she refused to say anything. At that point, he felt he had to force her to talk and keep her away from the rest of you. So he tied her up and stuck her in one of the houses until he could figure out what to do."

"What about HABITAT?" Tessa asked. "Is the whole organization involved."

Thomas shook his head. "No, your construction supervisor Debra did not know about it. The big boss Daniel Chickens can speak for himself."

Chickens was nearby, listening. "I'm in shock. I've known Badger for years and never thought he was capable of this. We're going to need better background checks and more people involved in selecting residents. As an organization, we are so sorry for what occurred. It will not happen again. I promise.'

"I plan to hold you to that," Toots McShae said. "OSHA will be watching you."

* * *

The next several months at HABITAT went smoothly. There were few glitches and little drama. All thirty tiny houses were completed.

The final volunteer party of the year was a lot of fun. Tessa even kissed Bobby and promised to visit if she was ever in Yolo County.

"Remember," he said, encouragingly, "our motto in Yolo County is: You Only Live Once."

* * *

Bobby entered high school. The first day, his history teacher, asked about his experience. "Tell us, Bobby, what are your thoughts about HABITAT and the Teen Emancipation Act."

Bobby stood up, considering the question. "How can I describe a year in which we learned to build houses, lived in a funky hotel, exposed a pickpocket ring, got by with no parents and no phone, and made great friends?" He shrugged, looking around the room at his classmates. "It was freaking awesome!"

FIVE ALBUMS

James W. Poindexter

I

The bedroom was cheerful and neat. The colors were soothing: apricot walls, white ceiling and tan carpet. Morning light poured through the window. You could imagine the person lying in bed waking to a summer day. Sadly, this was Greenbriar Skilled Nursing and my mother was dying.

"Is that you, Thomas?" she asked, her voice sounding croaky.

"Yeah, mom, it's me," I said, taking a seat near the bed.

Her illness had not been sudden. A year ago, after a lengthy round of chemo, she had fought off throat cancer. The family had celebrated with a party. Then, recently, her cancer returned, this time in her lungs. Treatment was pointless. Doctors shook their heads. *What can you expect after a half century of cigarettes.*

The local Hospice was managing her care. They had offered a spiritual advisor. She had said *No*. She was not a big fan of the afterlife.

"What about Dr. MacDougall?" I had reminded her. Back in 1907, Dr. Duncan MacDougall claimed to have weighed a body before and after death and, finding that the corpse was twenty-one grams lighter, concluded that the missing weight must be the *soul* now gone on to its reward.

"MacDougall was a *doofus*!" she had replied.

Hospice had also offered morphine, which she had likewise declined. She had no interest in spending her last weeks in a muddled haze.

Terminal disease is a *pain in the ass* (her words). She had stopped smoking and was suffering through bouts of pain. In return, she hoped for a revelation, some kind of epiphany. "I expected more," she had confided one day. "It's bad enough dying. Do I have to be disappointed too?"

For a literary person, she could be very practical. "Why can't we just die in our sleep?" she'd mused. "No lengthy illness, just a random, pre-assigned date. Boom! You're gone." Terminal illness was like bad theater. "Drop the curtain, already!"

Theater was her domain. She had spent her life writing plays, acting, painting sets and doing publicity. She always wanted us to join in. When we were young, she would drag us to set-building parties or read us her lines. "There are *thousands* of ways to support the theater," she'd say. "Talent is not required!" This last admonition had been directed at me, since Charlie and Isabel were natural performers.

We're a small family. Just mom, my sister, Isabel, and my older brother, Charlie. Charlie is no longer with us. He died a year ago in a bike accident. It had been a hit and run. They found him and his mangled bike in a grassy ditch by the road.

My sister Isabel is a theatrical agent in New York. She's busy and seldom gets back to California. Charlie had also had a successful career, publishing theatrical works. I was good with my hands and became a contractor. My wife, Stella, is a first grade teacher. We have two kids, Lisa, 6, and Wade, 5.

"I brought your mail," I said, placing the envelopes on the side table by the bed.

This had been our daily routine since her recent diagnosis. I retrieved the mail from her house in San Gabriel and brought it to her room at Greenbriar Skilled Nursing.

She had lived in the San Gabriel house for twenty-five years, ever since her divorce from my dad. The divorce was awful. Charlie sided with dad, while Isabel and I supported mom.

My dad had remarried and had another son, Larry. Charlie had stayed close with my dad and had made some effort to get to know his younger half-brother Larry, though with limited success.

When my dad heard about mom's latest illness, he had said, "Give her my *best*." I wasn't sure what that meant, so I said, "Dad says hi."

"A man of few words," she grunted. Perhaps, that had been their problem. She was a *gusher* when it came to words, while he kept his inner-thoughts to himself.

The nerve center of mom's house was her office. Other than the desk, it harbored stacks of paper, file cabinets, framed playbills and signed photos of actors. She had written over fifty plays. Most had been performed, mainly in Los Angeles, but some in New York. After watching her plays, you departed the theater feeling unchained, free to choose your own destiny.

I pushed the button to lift the head of her bed. She glanced at the stack of mail.

"Read one to me," she said.

I thumbed through the pile. There were solicitations, utility bills and several *get well* cards. "Here's one from Greta," I said. Greta had been a life-long friend, a sorority sister at Cal, a fellow actor, playwright and world traveler. Like Auntie Mame, Greta held the view that *Life is a banquet, and most poor sons-of-bitches are starving to death!*

"What does she say?" mom asked.

On the front of the card, Greta had drawn purple violets, mom's favorite flower. "Some violets," I said, showing her the picture.

Inside, Greta had written "*Darling Patience*". Mom's closest friends called her by her actual name *Patience*. Most people go by nicknames. For her, it was the opposite. Strangers tended to call her *Pat* or *Patty*, thinking that they were being familiar. Her inner circle, however, knew her as *Patience*.

Of course, *Patience* didn't suit her at all. She was far from patient. *Frenetic* would have been more apt. She had tried to make peace with her name. She had even embroidered *Patience is a virtue* on to a pillow. The pillow sat, as a reminder, on her sofa. But no amount of urging could undo her given disposition. She was destined to be a fidgety consumer of cigarettes, coffee and conversation.

Once upon a time, many girls had been named for the Virtues. Pope Gregory I, had centuries ago defined them as: *chastity, temperance, charity, diligence, kindness, patience and humility,* which were in constant battle with the seven Sins: *lust, gluttony, greed, sloth, envy, wrath, and pride*. According to mom, most of us are a mixture of both, namely, in her words, *virtuous sinners*.

I read aloud from Greta's card. "I've heard you're back in nursing care. I had my own bout with C last year but they say I'm okay, at least for now. I love you and I'm rooting for you!" She could put a positive spin on a sour situation.

Mom attempted a smile. "What's Greta doing these days?"

"She says she's in Palm Springs volunteering for Modernism Week."

Mom shook her head. "You know, back in the 60s, the architecture looked cheap, just flat roofs, straight lines and aluminum glass doors. Now, it's praised as *Mid-Century* and honored with its own *Modernism Week*!"

"Every dog has its day," I replied, with a shrug.

Mom suddenly grimaced. Her face was ashen. An alarm sounded from the equipment behind the bed. A nurse entered the room and rushed over.

II

By the next day, mom had recovered somewhat. But nothing could stem the tide. The cancer was invading her lungs, making it difficult to breathe and reducing oxygen to the brain.

"Hi mom," I said, entering her room. "How're you feeling today?"

She was weary, but in fair spirits. "Let's read from this play," she said, handing me a dog-eared script.

I looked at the cover page: *The Five Albums, a Play in Three Acts, by Patience Hansen.* I remembered the play. It was about the Austens, a prominent family in 1870s Pittsburgh. The family's luminaries of that era included a senator, bank president, physician and professor. In the play, the senator's wife, one Abigail Austen, sets out to document the family history and preserve its legacy.

The play's three acts follow generations of Austens, first in Pittsburgh (1875), then in Minneapolis (1912) and finally in Los Angeles (1972). The family's fortunes decline over time, eventually reduced to rags and ruin.

"Read the opening part to Act I," mom prompted. "I've marked the section in blue pencil. I'll be Abigail Austen and you can be Roger Wiener, her lazy, good-for-nothing brother."

I frowned. "I'm nothing like Robert Wiener," but then obliged her and began reading aloud.

> "The Austen parlor, high ceilinged, ornate chandelier, Victorian grandeur. Heavy, upholstered furniture. Tapestry and artwork hang on walls. Upstage, a bust of Caesar stands on a pedestal. Abigail, the wife of Senator Austen, in high collared dress, sits upright in a chair. Her brother, Roger Wiener, in velvet waistcoat, looking dissolute, lies on a sofa, rather bored.
>
> Roger: I don't understand the fuss. You weren't even born into this family. You're a *Wiener*!
>
> Abigail: You are so dull, Roger! The point is to preserve the *Austens*' history. I mean, who cares about *Wieners?*
>
> Roger: But why you? You used to be such fun! (Roger huffs, and inhales a pinch of snuff.)

Abigail: Someone has to do it. My husband and his brothers are too busy to attend to such things.

Roger: Zounds! It's not like they're Lincoln or Grant or even *demi-personages. Mon Dieu*! (He hiccups.) If they matter so much, a real historian will write about them someday. Then *all the world shall knowest thy glory!*

Abigail: You're such a killjoy! (She frowns.) This is a *family* album. I want to tell their story so future Austens know they come from *good stock*.

Roger: Do Americans really care which Neanderthal they descend from? Some of us are trying to forget.

Abigail: Of course, they do. Why, every religion has an origin story. It explains why we're here on earth. Why shouldn't a family know where it comes from?

Roger: Alright, I'll play along. What form would this chronicle take?

Abigail: I'm thinking a family album in perhaps five volumes, including photographs and biographies.

Roger: Why *five* volumes? Seems a bit random.

Abigail: Don't be silly! Nobody can be expected to look through more than five volumes. There's a *limit* to our powers of concentration!

Roger: Zounds! I feel weary thinking about it! Just imagine the readers' excitement when they see, *Robert Austen, Bank President, - pinched pennies while pitching penuriousness!*

Abigail: Really, Roger, you say *Zounds* far too often. Obviously, the point would be to present the family in an interesting light while emphasizing their successes.

Roger: Might I be mentioned?

Abigail: I'm not sure. Perhaps, in a footnote. See, Roger Wiener, *the sometimes amusing brother of Abigail Austen*.

The first act continues in this vein. Abigail assembles the initial album, complete with photos and lengthy descriptions of the current generation of Austens.

In a later scene, Abigail is showing the family album to Roger in the parlor.

Abigail: What do you think?

Roger: (Flipping pages of the first volume.) Rather dramatic, don't you think? Reads a bit like the *Odyssey*, full of heroics. Where are the normal people?

Abigail: *Mercy*! I want to show what this generation of Austens has accomplished. The point is to inspire, to instill pride. People want to learn about *heroes*, not some *average Joe.*

Roger: *Blimey!* I find *success* to be an utter bore. (He points to the bust of Caesar). Do kings and emperors really make the rest of us feel better? I prefer David Copperfield to Queen Victoria.

Abigail: Really, Roger, you say *blimey* far too often. When it comes to public *personae*, I prefer the pomp of a coronation over the work-a-day lot of the *everyman*.

Roger: (Changing the subject.) I notice you omitted the Austens who remained in Carolina and fought for the Confederacy. Rather arbitrary, what?

Abigail: The aim is to tell *this* family's story. *The Austens of Pennsylvania.* Why tarnish it?

Roger: Aha! I get it. Let the future generations know they descend from gods! Not complex, emotional gods, like the Greeks or Romans, but faultless, glorious beings. A family of *winners*, indeed!

Abigail: (Laughing in spite of herself.) Oh, Roger! You're such a pill."

I could tell mom was getting tired. "Let's stop for a while," I said.

"Yes," she said. "My point in the play was that the glorification of ancestors can kill future progress. If you think you descend from gods, where to go from there?"

"Yeah, I remember," I said. "Despite Abigail's intentions, the albums have the opposite effect. Instead of inspiring, they become a curse, haunting and crippling future generations. By the end of the third act, the family is nearly destitute."

"Well, I tried to end it on a positive note."

"Right," I said, recalling that, in the closing scene, Anne Austen, the teenage daughter, tosses the family album into the fireplace. "She says '*Ashes to ashes*' hoping the family is freed from the chains of its past glory." It was certainly a dramatic moment. "So why bring it up now?"

In a whisper, she said, "Go to the house and get our family photo albums. You'll find them by my desk."

III

Back at mom's house, I rummaged around the den and found the Hansen Family album on a shelf. Like the play, this album had five volumes, including photos, news clippings and biographical info going back one hundred and fifty years.

The desk phone rang. It was mom's landline. "Hello?"

"Mr. Hansen?"

"Yes?"

"It's Gina Smith at the Greenbriar. I'm afraid your mother is gone."

"Gone?"

"She passed. It happened soon after you left."

I drove back to the Greenbriar, carrying the Hansen Family album. As I entered the room, I could see her, eyes closed, still lying in bed.

I brought the album," I said to nobody in particular, turning slightly to show the volumes under my arm. I wasn't ready to say goodbye. "What the hell, mom?"

I sat in a chair by the bed. Late afternoon shadow had moved across the room. I called my wife Stella and my sister Isabel. Soon Hansens and Hansen-adjacent folks would be talking. I called mom's former agent and her friend Greta. It seemed so business like, like a sports commentary, *Mom loses in final quarter of tight game.*

Hospice had me sign some forms. The mortuary arrived. Mom's body was removed. Everybody was kindly. Even then, I remained in the room. Perhaps her soul had lingered, as Dr. MacDougall had predicted, waiting for instructions.

I wasn't ready to leave. I switched on a light and began leafing through the first volume of our family album. A sheet of paper fell to the floor. I picked it up. It was a letter.

"Thomas, each generation of our family has had an archivist who is responsible for editing and adding to the Hansen family album. I had that responsibility and, if you're reading this, you are my designated successor."

I'd seen the family album before, but it had been several years. I had no idea there was an *official archivist*. I'd never heard of such a thing. I continued reading:

"The rules are simple. First, as archivist, you must limit the album to no more than five volumes. In other words, if you add new material

(say about my life, heaven forbid!), you will have to cut from some other entry (like your great uncle Cleo the bank robber, ha ha!). Second, you must make the album available to family members for a limited time on request, but make sure they return it!"

I had noticed, pasted to the front cover of each volume, a kind of check-out sheet, like at a library, with names and dates. Presumably, these were family members who had requested the album in the past. Some of the dates were a hundred years ago or more. I kept reading:.

"If you're reading this letter, it also means I failed to solve the mystery described at the end of volume five. Frankly, I don't see how you (or I in my time) can move on without first solving this crime, if it was one. It has made my past year a torment. I had hoped to solve it without involving you. But, alas, here we are.

Oh, and tell Isabel not to take offense. I'm naming you the archivist because (how to put this nicely) you seem to have more free time to actually commit to the task. Anyway, sorry I'm not there to help, but hey it could be fun! And I love you of course. Bye."

There was a postscript:

"P.S. Remember my play, ***The Five Albums****. Don't use our family album to create heroes or, equally bad, to shame future generations for not measuring up to their ancestors. There are no meaningless lives, only poor historians. Avoid censure as much as coronation. There's a spark to every life."*

Eventually, I stood up, took a final look at the room, and left.

Stella had made fish tacos for dinner. My kids, Lisa and Wade, ate without much conversation. They had liked their grandma, though at five and six, they didn't feel the loss as acutely. I excused myself and went off to bed.

IV

"Dammit," I shouted, to nobody in particular. That morning, I had started reading volume one of the Hansen Family album.

"What is it?" Stella called from the other room.

As *archivist*, I couldn't see any easy way to edit what I'd read so far. The entries were already terse. Somehow, I would have to find room to add my mother's photos and tell her story. "I'm no good at this!" I complained.

"You'll find a way," Stella replied, encouragingly, without asking me what I was talking about.

The entries, and there were hundreds of them, were already bare-bones (forgive the pun). For example, one of our first ancestors in the New World was described as follows:

Norman Hansen, b. 1861 (Bergen, Norway), d. 1893 (Pierre, South Dakota). Left Norway 1867 with parents due to famine in northern Europe. Settled in Dakota Territory. Grain farmers. Married, Helga Johansen. They had five children of which three survived, Helga, Norman and Olav. Pastimes: played hardangar fiddle, Norse folk music. Succumbed to rheumatic fever at age 32.

Below the entry was a weathered black and white photo of a man in a dark wool suit sitting on a buckboard, with a plain white church in the background. On the next page, there was an entry for Norman Hansen's younger sister Emma.

Emma Hansen, b. 1873 (Dakota Territory), d. 1927 (Minneapolis, MN). Indentured to farm as servant until 21 yrs of age. Married Thomas Crowell. Grade school teacher, Minneapolis public schools. Three children, Robert, James and Madeline. Pastimes: reading, piano.

The entry was accompanied by a photograph of a cheerful looking woman in a striped jacket, striking cheek bones and dark hair piled up in a bun.

And so it went, page after page, entries and a few photos, all of them in the same terse style.

I turned to volume five to see if this pattern continued. I saw an entry for my great-grandfather. I'd met him when I was five and had a vague memory of him.

Harold Hansen, b. 1889 (Minneapolis, MN), d. 1983 (San Rafael, CA). Univ. of Minnesota (B.S. 1911), m. Ruth Magnusen (1918, Madison, WI). U.S. Army (1917-1919). Moved to Kentfield, CA (1919). Logging camps (Yosemite) railroad construction (Alaska). Real estate management. Army Corps of Engineers (Nike missile bases). Pastimes: deep-sea fishing and gardening.

There was a photo of Harold Hansen in a canoe somewhere in the Boundary Waters of Minnesota. He looked like an outdoorsman, accustomed to bad climates and big bugs.

"What do you think?" Stella asked, breaking through my reverie.

"I don't know. It reminds me of a memorial wall, like that Vietnam Memorial in D.C. There are name after name, lives lived and lost. I thought I'd feel a connection but it's like they're strangers. At least the older ones.

"Well, at least you know the connections that lead to you. That's more than I can say."

"I guess that's the best way to look at it. It's really a history of people falling in love. If A had not met B then C would never have been born, and so on."

"Right. I think that was your mom's point. It shouldn't be about blood or genetics. There's little point in saying *my family's better than yours*, since humans share 99.9% of the same DNA."

I had noticed that the album did not emphasize fame or celebrity. Unlike mom's play, *The Five Albums*, the album downplayed those kinds of accomplishments. "Yes, the past archivists have made a point of describing loving relationships rather than trying to chronicle bragging rights," I said.

Stella was nodding. "I agree with that approach to these family histories. There's not much joy in saying you're Taylor Swift's cousin, if that's all you're remembered for."

In my lifetime, the world's population has grown from 3 billion to 8 billion people, all of whom may have had a common ancestor. However, given the sheer numbers, we seem to have lost track of how we are inter-related.

I didn't fool myself that the people in the Hansen Family album were any better or worse than other people. As I read through the initial volumes, the entries seemed to reflect real people, sinners and saints alike. Up to that point, I had no idea what *mystery* awaited me at the end of volume five.

V

Mom's instructions were clear: *I want a green burial, no embalming, stick me in a cotton sack, in the ground, and let me rot.* A few L.A. cemeteries offered that service. We had selected *Green Acres*, in the Glendale foothills. It didn't look like a cemetery. There were no head stones or monuments. In fact, it resembled an open field with a few oaks and sycamores scattered about.

Isabel flew in from New York. She, Stella, my kids and I were standing next to a hole in the grassy field. *Green Acres*' used a horse drawn cart to carry the body to the site.

"Amish vibe," Isabel said. "Mom would have liked that."

I nodded.

There was no priest or rabbi. When asked about her religious preference, mom had always said *None.* Of the 4,000 religions identified by *Wikipedia*, none of them had resonated. One time, she said, "When you're an ant, you see your ant hill as the universe. Human religion is like that. We can't imagine the magnitude of existence. It's too scary."

"She wanted to go back to the earth," Isabel said.

I nodded again.

The cemetery staff lowered her body into the grave. They shoveled dirt back into the hole, then replaced the sod. The burial site was again part of a grassy field. The morning was merging into afternoon. I was having trouble imagining a world without her. I reached for Stella's hand. My chest pounded and my eyes stung. As we walked across the field, back to the car, I wondered how many people might be under foot.

We were soon back in Pasadena. It was a sunny day. The San Gabriel mountains to the north were clearly visible. We decided to sit outside on the redwood deck.

"What have you been up to?" Isabel asked me.

I told Isabel about the family album. She was surprised by the five volume limit. "Why not a thousand pages and post it in the cloud?" she asked.

"Well," I started to explain, "if it's too long, whether paper or digital, nobody will read it. I think the goal, as I understand it, is to review it in one sitting. It should be fun, not a research project."

"So you need to shorten some entries in order to add new ones, like for mom?"

"Yes, that's part of it," I said, "but I think your idea is a good one. We could keep the original five volumes but also provide references to a website if someone wants more detail. For example, we could scan and post some of mom's plays if anyone was interested in reading them."

"You should scan and post the current album anyway," she suggested.

"But, first, I want to add an entry for mom."

"Shouldn't be a problem," she said, smiling. "It's not like she did much."

I laughed, which felt good.

"I'm going back to New York in the morning," she said. "Lots to do."

I paused, wondering whether to share with her the mystery that I'd discovered. "Would you stay a few more days? There's something I want to show you."

VI

"Incredible!" Isabel said, reading the file that our mother had slipped in at the end of the Hansen Family album. "She thought Charlie was murdered?"

"She was obviously investigating his death." I had read the file. In addition to her notes, she had obtained evidence from the L.A.P.D. and Highway Patrol. The documents included accident reports, autopsy findings, photographs of the scene, and some witness statements. Unfortunately, there had been no eye witness to the accident itself.

"I wonder why?" she asked.

"Look at the last page of the album. Do you see the final entry there for Charlie?" I waited for her to find the entry. "Under *Cause of Death* she wrote *bike accident ???*"

Isabel nodded. "Mom was questioning how Charlie died."

"She had suspicions about Larry, our half-brother. She even called dad. He told her that, under his will, Larry and Charlie would share in his estate. Larry was already envious of Charlie, probably competing for dad's affections."

“And money, I suppose,” added Isabel.

She and I never thought about dad’s wealth since we had severed ties with him years ago. Charlie, on the other hand, had kept close with dad and had even tried to befriend his younger half-brother.

I continued. “According to mom’s theory, during one of Charlie’s bike rides near Griffith Park, Larry had followed him by car and, when the opportunity arose, had run him over.”

“Is there any evidence to link Larry to the accident?”

“Mom hired a private investigator to research Larry’s car, a BMW. He found out the car had been repaired around that time.”

“Why not check with CARFAX?”

“Body damage won’t show up in CARFAX unless there’s an insurance claim or police report. Hit and run accidents aren’t reported. Anyway, the PI obtained an invoice from Dinelli’s Auto Body. The invoice showed that, one week after Charlie’s death, Larry had repairs done to the BMW’s front right bumper and headlight.”

“Did mom share any of this with the police?”

“I don’t think so. By then, she was dealing with her health issues.”

“So, who was the investigating officer?”

“The report says it was a Sergeant Jake Silva.”

“Let’s call him up."

We contacted Sergeant Silva and made an appointment to see him later that day. In the meantime, we decided to visit Larry where he worked. He was a floor manager at the Macy’s on Santa Monica Blvd.

Late morning traffic was light and we arrived before noon. We walked through the men’s department and spotted Larry helping a cashier with a credit issue. We stood by until he finished.

“Larry?” I said.

He turned toward us. “Oh, hi guys. What are you doing here?” he asked, a bit warily.

“Oh, we were in the neighborhood,” Isabel replied, “Thought we’d let you know in person that our mom passed away this week.”

“Sorry to hear that,” he said, even though he’d only spoken to our mom once or twice. “Anything I can do for you?”

“No, we have it covered. There won’t be a service. Just a burial in a field in the foothills.”

Larry was looking impatient. “Well, good seeing you,” he said, starting to turn away.

“Hey Larry,” I blurted, “mind if I ask you a question about Charlie?” Before he had a chance to respond, I continued. “We still have some questions about how he died. Did you or dad ever look into that at all?”

“Just an accident as far as we knew. They never tracked down the driver.”

I was about to ask another question, when Larry looked at his watch and nervously pivoted away. “Sorry, I really have to get back to work.”

We watched him go.

“He seems anxious,” Isabel said.

“Yeah.”

We had time for lunch before our two o’clock meeting with Sergeant Silva. After lunch, we headed over to the West Traffic Division on Venice Blvd. We were shown to Silva’s cubicle.

“Good afternoon,” he said, pleasant but gruff.

"Thanks for seeing us," Isabel said, smiling. Unlike me, she had good people skills. We agreed that she should take the lead. "We wondered about the status of the investigation into Charlie's death."

"Nothing new, I'm afraid," said Silva.

Isabel explained that our mom had looked into Charlie's accident. She gave Silva a copy of the file. "She hired a PI. He found out that our half-brother Larry had body work done to his BMW the week after Charlie's death."

"What reason would Larry have for harming Charlie?" Silva asked.

She explained the situation with our dad's will and how Larry would benefit if Charlie were not around.

Silva examined the repair invoice and photos the PI had obtained from the repair shop. "Well, that damage is consistent with some sort of accident."

Silva promised to talk to Larry and take another look at the accident. We thanked him and went on our way.

Later that afternoon, back at my house, my phone rang. I put it on speaker. "Hi dad."

"Sorry to hear about your mom," he began. "You could have called me directly rather than springing it on Larry at work."

It wasn't worth arguing the point. "Sorry, yes, she died. It was fortunately pretty quick."

"I don't appreciate your bringing up Charlie's accident again. I thought we were over that," dad scolded. "Please don't harass Larry about these things."

"Well, now that you bring it up, mom said your estate was to go to Charlie and Larry. Now that Charlie's gone, I assume Larry gets his share?"

The phone went dead.

"Way to smooth things over," Isabel scolded.

"At least we shook things up."

"I'm heading home tomorrow," Isabel said. "You can call me if anything comes up."

VII

A couple days later, Sergeant Silva called me. "We think the Larry angle is a dead end."

I felt disappointed. I'd been hoping for mom's sake that her investigation would pan out. "What did you find out?"

"Larry was in an accident, that much was true. But it was over on La Brea on his way to work. Both he and the other driver reported it. I have the insurance claims. Nothing there."

"What about my father's estate?"

"Larry doesn't get any more because of Charlie's death. Charlie's share is now going to the L.A. County Bicycle Coalition. At least, that's what your father says."

"So, we're dead in the water. We'll never know who did this to Charlie?"

"Not exactly," he said. There was a pause. "Your inquiry got me thinking. What if this wasn't a hit and run at all? So we ran some further tests."

"And?"

"The soil we found in the soles of Charlie's shoes and on his pants did not match the soil at the site."

"Meaning?"

"The body was moved."

This was creeping me out. "You mean he was killed elsewhere?"

"Yes."

"Anything else?"

"We found traces of tire rubber in multiple locations on the bike but not on Charlie's clothes."

"Somebody ran over the bike?"

"Which makes no sense if this was a typical *car vs. bike* accident. In other words, the damage to the bike occurred independently from the injuries to Charlie."

"What are you saying?" I asked, bewildered. "Someone killed Charlie, then damaged his bike, then put the two together up at Griffith Park to make it look like a hit and run?"

"That's the size of it. We're referring the matter to Robbery-Homicide."

The call left me shaken. A hit and run is one thing. An intentional murder is another. The idea that somebody had killed Charlie then staged a bike accident seemed bizarre. I called Isabel.

Isabel said, "Mom had that sixth sense. She knew there was more to Charlie's death."

"Now that it's a murder, maybe they'll dig into it," I said.

VIII

A few weeks later, I received a call from Sergeant Silva.

"We have some news," he said. "Charlie wasn't murdered, at least in the usual sense."

"What was it?"

"Well, it was road rage," he said. "A witness came forward. Charlie was biking on Los Feliz Blvd. when he was hit. We think the driver had been drinking. He put Charlie and the bike in his car, then restaged the accident up in Griffith Park."

"Why would he do that?" I asked.

"I don't know. He told the witness he was taking Charlie to the hospital to get checked out. We expect Charlie was already dead."

"So he dumps Charlie and the bike in a ditch and drives away?"

"That's about the size of it. Like I said, he was probably drunk. Maybe he thought it would give him plausible deniability."

"What did he say, when you confronted him?"

"You know, he initially went on about how he had no reason to be in the Park since his route was on Los Feliz Blvd. But, when the lab found Charlie's blood in the car and residue from the car's tire on the bike, as well as soil samples from Los Feliz that were a match to the soil in Charlie's shoes, well, the guy confessed to the whole thing."

"Did he have some explanation? I mean, why Charlie?"

"You know, the usual stuff. It was early morning. He was coming home late from an all night poker party. Charlie was riding his bike in the lane of traffic. The guy got mad and gunned it."

"What was his name?"

"You won't believe it."

"Try me."

"Elmer Fudd."

"Really?"

"Yeah, that was the guy's real name. We have him in custody."

IX

A few days after that revelation, I was working on the family album, finally adding an entry for my mother and completing the entry for Charlie. It had not been difficult to find space. I had found a double entry for one of our ancestors. After deleting the duplication, there was ample room for my inserts without violating the *five volume* limit.

My daughter Lisa was watching me. “What are you doing?” she asked.

“Oh, I’m working on the family album. Adding a piece about your grandma.”

She appeared confused. “What’s a family album?”

I wasn’t sure how to answer. “I guess it’s a collection of photos and stories about your family. It’s about the people who love you, or who loved the people who love you. Does that make sense?”

“I guess.” She shrugged. “What are you writing about Nana.

“Lots of stuff. She was a writer. She lived her life like she was on a stage, and every word, motion and silence mattered.”

“I miss her.”

“Me too, sweetie.”

And, in that moment, I thought about Dr. MacDougall’s experiment. How excited he must have been in 1907 when he thought he’d found clear evidence of the soul. How else to explain the loss of weight during the transition from life to death?

I suppose some part of us does pass from one generation to the next. And maybe that’s the point of a family album, to share with each generation a sense of our virtues and sins, successes and failures. Perhaps it keeps us from becoming too arrogant, or too depressed.

We know so little about ourselves. However, I felt certain of one thing: Patience was a virtue.

SEA OF CORTEZ

James W. Poindexter[1]

Vera Cruz was lying in the bottom of a small panga boat. It offered no protection against the afternoon sun. Her face was burned and her lips were chapped. There was no sound except of water lapping against the hull. Far off, in her dream, she heard her father's voice. *Mija, despiértete! Wake up!*

She tried to move. There was a painful lump on her head and her long black hair was sticky with drying blood. As a child in Mexico City, she had once fallen from a bike onto a cobbled street. The fall had given her a concussion. Her father had called her *pobrecita*. This felt much worse.

She inventoried her few possessions: clothes, shoes, wedding ring, earrings, gold chain, watch and glasses. Her phone and wallet were missing. According to her watch, it was three o'clock on May 25. More than a day had passed since her last memory.

She pulled herself up onto the rowing bench. There were no oars. She crawled clumsily toward the stern. An outboard motor hung off the transom. The motor merely gasped when she pulled the cord. The

---

1 Adapted from the novel, *Vera Cruz: Borderland Boogie*, James W. Poindexter (2024)

gas tank was empty. In every direction, there was only water and sky. She was alone.

Her last memories of Mazatlán were of the one-eyed man, the giant they called *Cyclops.* He had reportedly lost an eye in a knife fight, while employed by the DEA. Since then, he had become a *consultant*, working mostly in Mexico, for a mix of clients - government, cartel, business - whoever could pay his fee.

She had asked him, "How do you get away with it, working for different sides?"

Cyclops had laughed at that. "I don't have a conflict of interest, only an interest in conflict." He was clever. She had to give him credit for that. But mostly, the man was drawn to violence and, where none existed, he fomented it. He had bragged, "I can trigger a riot in a Mexican village then organize the vigilantes to shoot down the rioters."

She was suddenly angry at herself. A bookish lawyer, thirty-five years old, she had no business confronting this monster. She was lucky he hadn't killed her. However, considering her situation, she thought, *maybe he had.*

She tried to recreate the events since yesterday. She was wearing dark pants and a white shirt and had on rubber soled shoes. Everything felt damp. Examining the motor, it was obvious the rudder handle had been fixed in place by a length of rope. Cyclops, she assumed, had knocked her out, thrown her in the boat, started the motor and pointed her out to sea.

She gazed out over the water. It was turquoise-gray and relatively calm. She assumed it was the Sea of Cortez. If it had been the Pacific, the small boat would have been swamped. The boat had traveled northwest from Mazatlán, perhaps two hundred miles before running out of gas.

She knew the circumstances were dire: no food or water, no shelter and no means of navigation other than the wind and tides. Except for her service in the Mexican army, she had always lived in the city and was ill-equipped for survival.

At least it's the Sea of Cortez, she thought, trying to console herself. She dipped her hand into the water. It was warmer than the Pacific.The Baja peninsula shielded the Sea of Cortez from the cold water that drifted from Canada down the west coast, the so-called California Current.

Her father would have said, *Tranquila amor! Stay calm.* She still remembered his voice, resonant and soothing. Two years ago, when he was dying, he had said, "Don't worry, mija, the people you love will stick with you even after they're gone." He had always been there for her in hard times.

Her meeting with Cyclops had started innocently enough. It was meant to be a simple exchange of information. DEA sources had arranged the meeting. The two of them had met just before dawn at Olas Altas beach in Mazatlán. Cyclops had offered to provide facts about the border crimes she was investigating.

It had made little sense for *her* to meet with Cyclops. She was a deputy with the Mexico Attorney General's Office and, typically, she did not handle field work. Her time was mostly spent in her Mexico City office, surrounded by law books and files. Nonetheless, her boss, Carlos Fuentes, the assistant AG, had asked her to investigate certain crimes at the border. In particular, she had been looking into the violent death of a Nuevo Laredo police officer, Mariano Azuela.

“Why did we have to meet here?” she had asked, glancing around her. The beach was dark and foreboding.

“People are looking for me,” he had said. “It’s better this way."

She shrugged. “What can you tell me about the Azuela killing in Nuevo Laredo?”

Cyclops had seemed surprised by the question. “I thought you wanted to know something about the cartels. How would I know about a dead cop?” He had sounded perturbed.

“Take it easy,” she had said, calmly. “One of the DEA guys told me you were in Nuevo Laredo at the time. I thought you might have heard something.” At that point in their conversation, she thought the meeting would be a bust.

The water sparkled in the afternoon sun. There were no landmarks, no streets, cars or people to fill the space, only swaths of blue and gray. It was nothing like life in Mexico City which was extravagantly busy with color and detail. In the city, the mind was constantly jumping from one thing to the next, thousands of times a day.

She stared at the sky, then the water, then back at the sky. Someone had told her, *we only see the light reflected from things and not the things themselves*. She had thought at the time that human senses were adequate to find food and shelter and distinguish friend from foe. However, here, on the Sea of Cortez, her senses were offering no information of value.

She had persisted in her interview of Cyclops. “What were you doing at the border anyway? I mean, why were you in Nuevo Laredo.”

“You don’t really want to know,” he’d said.

She had encouraged him to answer.

"Okay," he had said, "but you're not going to like it."

"Tell me."

Cyclops hesitated, then said, "An American client of mine wanted to stir things up on the Mexican side of the border, then blame it on the cartels. They hoped to start a war. Anyway, I helped stage some crimes that were supposed to be a catalyst for war and then planted evidence that pointed at the cartels."

"What kind of crimes?"

"Well, lots of things. I blew up portions of the border wall and arranged for a lot of cocaine and illegals to cross into the U.S. Homeland Security was notified. There were busts, with everything pointing back at the cartels. The plan seemed flawless. As you know, war nearly broke out for real."

She had been confused. "How would that benefit your clients?"

"Let me draw you a picture." he had said. "The cartels get blamed for these crimes, the U.S. demands that Mexico intervene, the Mexican army gathers at the border, violence ensues, the U.S. sends its own forces to protect its interests, battles rage across the border, the U.S. uses the occasion to march into northern Mexico quelling the riot, killing off the cartels and seizing their property and business. You get the idea."

The whole thing sounded insane. "Again, how would that benefit your clients?"

"That's easy. My clients were pharmaceutical companies. They wanted to take over the cartels' business, especially since the cartels' black market for fentanyl and other drugs directly competes with Big Pharma's own business. Once the U.S. army cleared the way, my clients - through some intermediaries - planned to absorb the cartels' operations."

"Why would the U.S. government help with such a plan?" she had asked, bewildered.

"Let's just say there are a lot of folks in the U.S. government who would like to see the border permanently closed and militarized, like East Berlin once was. Imagine a permanent U.S. military presence in Mexico with bigger walls, prison-like guard towers, armed drones, surveillance, facial recognition, all aimed at keeping people *out* of the U.S."

She had wanted to solve the murder of a border cop. According to Cyclops, the murder had been only part of an elaborate plan to incite a war.

Her mind was wandering. She was thirsty and couldn't concentrate. The boat was bobbing, moving with the tide, but in no clear direction. The Sea of Cortez was huge, as much as a hundred miles across and ten thousand feet deep. It had been formed when tectonic forces pulled the Baja peninsula away from the North American Plate and the Pacific had flowed into the resulting abyss. Like the tides, the earth's crust was in constant movement. There was no *terra firma.* People's sense of security while standing on *solid ground* was an illusion.

Her thoughts were interrupted when a giant manta ray flew over the stern of the boat. Soon, several other rays were airborne, soaring then belly-flopping onto the water's surface. They were huge creatures, ten or fifteen feet across and shaped like alien spacecraft. She imagined they were avoiding sharks or shedding parasites or hunting insects or simply playing. She welcomed the distraction. They were the first living things she'd seen.

She passed the remaining afternoon, drifting in and out of sleep, waiting for rescue or whatever might come.

Towards dusk, a dense fog rolled in. She felt chilled.

The fog cleared out during the night. Her watch battery had died, and she didn't know the time. A three-quarter moon rose in the east. The moonlight formed a fan-shaped beacon across the water. Something large, perhaps a whale, called in the distance. Hunger and fatigue lulled her back to sleep.

She woke to a sudden *crack!* The moon had disappeared. Clouds had gathered and winds kicked up waves against the small boat. There were lightning strikes to the west. The rain began, at first soft, then cold and pelting. She cupped her hands and drank. The water revived her. But, the boat was filling up. She used her hands to scoop out the water, barely staying ahead of the rain.

The next morning was calm. Her clothes were soaked. However, the temperature was rising and she no longer felt chilled. She removed her damp shirt and pants and hung them to dry. She then eased herself over the side and into the water. She swam in circles around the boat.

While swimming, she thought about the countless creatures, unseen, in the sea below her. In 1940, John Steinbeck had spent six weeks on the Sea of Cortez collecting specimens with his biologist friend Ed Ricketts. She had read *The Log from the Sea of Cortez* which recounted the journey. The sea had been called the *Aquarium of the World*, because of its diverse array of life from phytoplankton to whales.

She felt somewhat refreshed from the swim. She thought again about her father, who had raised her after her mother had died. He had worked for the Metro system in Mexico City, maintaining its equipment. His true passion, however, had been Mexican history. She wondered what he would have thought about the conspiracy Cyclops had described. Could the Americans really start such a war and confiscate the cartels' drug business?

She imagined him saying, "That border between the U.S. and Mexico is recent history. It didn't exist until 1848. Our ancestors had been here for thousands of years before that. President Polk declared war against Mexico. Relying on Manifest Destiny, the Americans wanted to acquire new territory and expand to the west. As you know, with the border created by the *Treaty of Guadalupe Hidalgo,* the U.S. ended up taking half of Mexico's land."

"And your point is?" she might have asked.

"That is the point, the Americans have done it before. When they want land, they take it. They preach human rights, until it interferes with their interests."

Her father had always seen the *Americanos* as newcomers to the continent. They were like nomadic gunslingers, basically lawless and eager to fight. Those discussions had sparked her interest in law school. She was curious about whether treaties, especially unjust treaties, could be invalidated.

She was beginning to see Cyclops as the embodiment of American zeal. He was brazen, almost medieval in his violence, a living example of *might equals right*. That was the irony of some people. They would never condone theft among their neighbors, but welcomed it as a nation, willing to justify taking another country's land by force. There were examples every day in the news.

Her father had told her, "You know, we named you Vera Cruz, as in the one *true cross,* not because we were Catholic, but because we wanted you to have faith in yourself and always seek the truth." She wasn't sure what the truth was anymore. History felt like an ocean tide, working its mischief, independent of human will. Somehow, it had cast her aside, mere flotsam on an open sea.

She had again asked Cyclops about Mariano Azuela.

"What about him?" he had responded, defensively.

"Well," she continued, "the officer's body was loaded onto a local plane in Nuevo Laredo and flown across the border into Texas. He was dropped onto a Laredo shopping mall. His body had been stuffed with a kilo of cocaine. It's the kind of thing somebody like you would have noticed."

Cyclops had said, "Gee, beats me," and turned to leave.

She had followed him. "Really? That's all you know?"

He had spun suddenly to face her. "What the hell do you want from me!"

"Just tell me what you know. How was Mariano Azuela killed?"

Cyclops had seemed to ponder the question, then suddenly made a decision. "You really want to know?"

She had nodded.

He had shrugged, then said, "It wasn't me. The governor of Tamaulipas State arranged to have the cop killed. Maybe Azuela knew the governor was working with the Americans to start a war at the border. Who knows? That's above my pay grade. Anyway, the

Americans asked me to pick up the cop's body in Nuevo Laredo, stuff him with the cocaine and drop him on the American side of the border. You know the rest."

She had been foolish for her to ask for those details. Having told her, Cyclops might feel obliged to stop her from sharing the information. Certainly, she had no business meeting with Cyclops in the first place. The whole thing had been a mistake.

Her life had been like that, a series of accidents, linked together by a winding path. She had met her husband Emilio at a community theater in Coyoacán where he happened to be performing. A friend had given her the ticket at the last moment.

Similarly, she had gotten her job with the AG's office after meeting the AG at a law conference. She had attended on the spur of the moment because a former professor thought she might be interested. Her meeting with Cyclops had followed the same pattern. She was like a ball in a pinball game careening from flipper to buzzer to bust. She wondered how anybody could believe in free will given the random forces at play.

Thinking about Cyclops was not getting her anywhere. Her prospects for survival were not good. She even wondered whether she was in fact still alive. And if she was alive, how could she prove it? After all, many cultures thought that death involved crossing water to a spirit world.

Water had symbolic value in nearly all religions. It was a symbol of cleansing and rebirth. For the Christians, there was the River Jordon and baptism. For the ancient Greeks, one crossed the River Styx on the way to the underworld. The Hindus believed the dead crossed the Vaitarani River and, for Japanese Buddhists, it was the Sanzu River.

Her own upbringing had exposed her to Catholic *and* Aztec beliefs. The Aztec underworld was known as Mictlán which, far from being a stationary place, actually involved a challenging multi-year journey through nine levels of trial and tribulation. One of the first tasks was to cross the treacherous Apanohuaya River. The Catholics, however, did not associate the afterlife with any particular body of water. Heaven was peaceful and hell was painful, but they were otherwise short on specifics. The Aztec afterlife, on the other hand, read like an adventure story.

When she was young, nearly everyone in Mexico had been Catholic and some of them followed native traditions as well. Religion offered an origin story and a purpose. Perhaps it was being close to death, but she was revisiting the state of her own spirituality. Her beliefs seemed to wane each year with the advances in science. With the loss of mystery, there was less room for faith.

The world had once been richly inhabited by gods, sorcerers, ghosts, mermaids, monsters, witches, alchemists and magicians. There were countless stories of encounters with such beings. Now, these creatures were the subject of children's cartoons and Marvel movies, entertaining but fundamentally bogus. One didn't hear about people encountering the Hulk or Captain Marvel.

Her mind was now fretting the effects of science, which had seemingly plunged the world into a kind of darkness. Miracles were hard to come by. Knowledge had conquered imagination. People were too eager to cede control of their lives to technology. She too was guilty of relying on apps for information. As human knowledge grew, human spirit dwindled. They were losing the tug of war with technology. Humans' fate on earth would soon be akin to that of God in a Joan Osborne song,

What if God was one of us?
Just a slob like one of us
Just a stranger on the bus
Tryin' to make his way home?

A haiku popped into her mind:

Science has slain myth,
and promptly will come for us,
will Siri advise?

Her thoughts were becoming stew-like, a mixture of ill-defined thoughts. She tried to focus.

Peering west across the water, she could imagine the coastline of Baja. During his voyage in 1532, Hernan Cortez had mistaken Baja for an island, naming it *California,* a reference to the mystical island in the *Adventures of Esplandian* (1510) by Garci Rodriguez de Montalvo. Like other Spanish conquistadores, Cortez had read the story about *Calafía*, a warrior queen who ruled the vastly rich fictional island of California, and who attacked Constantinople, then a Byzantine Christian stronghold, but was defeated by the knight Esplandian.

How many stories had there been of sea monsters, sirens and errant voyages. Her favorite had been the *Odyssey*. The parallels between her current plight and Odysseus were plain. Odysseus had blinded *his* Cyclops, Polyphemus, the son of Poseidon, who, as punishment, subjected Odysseus to endless misadventures as he tried to sail back to Ithaca. She had confronted *her* Cyclops and, as a result, was now lost at sea. *What other perils might await me*? she wondered.

The heat was overwhelming. She took off her shirt, soaked it and wrapped it around her head. The cool, wet linen gave her some relief.

In Mexico City, the Attorney General's Office was in an uproar. Officers Gato and Hernandez had been recalled for an urgent meeting with Assistant AG Carlos Fuentes.

"How the hell did you leave her alone?" Fuentes asked, glaring at Hernandez.

The *federale* looked crestfallen. "She insisted I take charge of the search for the Cyclops' accomplices." he said, sadly.

"Yeah, and how did that work out?" Fuentes responded.

"Not so good. We haven't found them," Gato offered.

"Right. And meanwhile, Vera's missing and Cyclops is still out there!"

"Look, we feel bad, just tell us what we can do," Hernandez replied.

"Well, one thing is, we need to alert U.S. Customs and the DEA to watch for Cyclops."

"Already done," Hernandez said.

"In the meantime," the Assistant AG added, "commit all our resources to Mazatlán. Find out where Vera went."

Vera's mind was increasingly in a dream state. She thought she had seen her husband, Emilio. *But wasn't he filming a telenovela in Vancouver?* She hadn't seen him in months. She also imagined talking to a friend, Juan Escribo, on a bench atop Chapultepec Hill in Mexico City. The huge park had once been a center of Aztec civilization high above Lake Texcoco. Back then, one would have seen causeways, marketplaces and pyramids taller than any European cathedrals. Juan was a teacher at Mexico's *National Institute of Anthropology and History*. He had spent a lifetime teaching and excavating for ancient relics and tombs. In her imagination, Juan kept repeating, *Where are you going, Vera?* She wasn't sure how to reply.

The final moments of her meeting with Cyclops came back to her. She had been eager to hear whatever information he could offer. Now she knew. Governor Cazadero was responsible for the border cop's death. She needed to pass that information to her team at the AG's office. She had turned to leave. Cyclops had said, "Hey, where are you going?"

"It's time to go," she had answered.

His face had darkened. "I don't think so."

She had felt her heart racing. "Look, they know I'm here."

"Not a problem," he'd said calmly, "you won't be here for long."

She could feel the tide pulling the boat, although she wasn't sure in what direction. The tides in the Sea of Cortez were dramatic, up to sixteen feet of vertical displacement. The hot sun and dehydration were eroding what little energy she had. Impulsively, she crawled to the edge of the boat and dropped into the water.

For a moment, she remained underwater, a foot below the surface. Her body tingled. She emerged only to see the boat twenty feet away. The gap was widening. She swam as best she could. For a moment, it seemed helpless. A sudden gust of wind caught the boat and pushed it towards her. She reached it and clumsily climbed in.

A cloud passed overhead and she felt a chill. Before long, her eyes closed and she slept.

Some time later, she woke, confused. It was dark and damp. Water was striking against the hull. She sat up, hoping to see lights or stars, but there was only a dense mist enshrouding the boat. She heard a moan, maybe a whale or the wind.

The lapping grew louder. The boat started to rock and then something enormous struck the side, flipping the boat and sending her toppling into the sea. She watched helplessly as the boat receded into the mist. She began to flail in the water. For several minutes she struggled. Then suddenly, her feet struck sand.

She followed the sand upward. Her head, then her shoulders rose above the water. She emerged onto a small beach and nearly collided with a fan palm. It was a bit warmer out of the water.

She walked from one side of the small beach to the other, back and forth, fighting off the chill. She called out, "Is anyone here?" The adrenaline was wearing off. She lay down on the beach and fell into a deep sleep.

It happened sometimes that, if she was especially tired, her father would appear in her dreams. This time, she could see him distinctly. He kept repeating *You'll be okay.*

She didn't know how much time had passed. She sensed a comb pressing, front to back, against her hair. She was on the beach, with her legs stretched in front of her. Her back was propped up as if leaning against someone's knees. A woman, was humming something, dirge-like, while braiding Vera's hair, first the left side, then the right.

"What are you doing?" Vera asked, trying to stay calm.

"Make you pretty." The woman replied, but not in Spanish.

"Is that Nahuatl, the Aztec language?" Vera asked. She knew some phrases but wasn't fluent. Yet, she seemed to understand what the woman was saying.

"Uh huh."

"Where am I?" Vera asked.

"Isla de los Muertos," the woman said.

Vera had never heard of that island in the Sea of Cortez. There was an Isla El Muerto close to the Baja peninsula, but she couldn't be that far west. Anyway, there were many islands whose names alluded to el diablo or la muerte, so the name did not particularly alarm her.

"What's your name?" Vera asked.

The woman was finishing the right braid as she said, "*Mictecacihuatl.*"

Vera tensed. She knew well that, in Aztec mythology, Mictecacihuatl was the goddess of death. The Día de los Muertos was the goddess' day. It had been observed in one form or another for centuries before the Spanish arrived.

"Why are you making me pretty?" Vera asked.

"For your passage," the woman said, vaguely.

Vera dug into her pants pocket and found her bifocals. She put them on. The beach was still in mist. Everything appeared in shades of gray, a monochrome. She shifted forward and turned to face the woman. She didn't know what to expect, perhaps a skeletal phantom or an ancient sorceress in tribal gown. She was relieved to see an older woman with a strong face and kind eyes. The woman was wearing a simple woven dress and sandals.

"You have beautiful hair," the woman said. "On the beach, I couldn't wake you. Hope you don't mind, I braided your hair."

"Of course," Vera replied, recalling childhood sleepovers, girls braiding hair, sharing stories. "Uh, I've had such a strange few days. I mean, sorry to be so awkward," Vera stammered. "Do you have any water or food?"

The woman reached into a coarse straw bag and removed some fruit and a small stone pitcher of water, and offered them.

Vera drank and ate. "Is there a way to the mainland?" Vera asked, pointing towards what she hoped was the east.

"Only by canoe. My brothers can take you, on the tide."

The circumstances were dreamlike. Vera felt almost weightless, like a vapor. *Am I experiencing some sort of metamorphosis,* she wondered. Other living things transitioned from land to air. She thought of a butterfly emerging from its chrysalis.

Some catalyst was at work, changing her. *Perhaps it was the concussion*, she thought, *or the woman's touch or the fruit or water*.

"May I braid *your* hair?" Vera offered, somehow finding the words in Nahuatl.

"Yes," Mictecacihuatl said, simply. She handed the comb to Vera.

Vera stared at the comb. It was carved from bone. "This looks very old," she said.

"Yes, from a gray whale."

It was late afternoon when Mictecacihuatl's two brothers arrived. They had broad faces, long dark hair and coal-colored eyes. They were very muscular beneath their loose, woven clothes. Each wore an amulet of some kind around his neck and a bracelet of carved shell or bone. Their canoe was maybe twenty feet long, and must have been carved from a single tree. They pointed for her to get in while they steadied each end of the canoe.

Vera held Mictecacihuatl's hands. "Thank you."

The older woman nodded, kindly. "Goodbye."

The canoe was buoyant and slid easily across the water. The fog remained and Vera was not sure how the men could navigate. Even so, they continued to row with firm strokes.

After several minutes, the canoe emerged from the fog. The sun was radiant and quickly dried the damp from her clothes. The men continued to row, in rhythm. Despite the clear day, the men's bodies retained the same misty outline, slightly blurred, as if they were out of focus. She gazed at her own hands. Each finger was distinct.

The canoe glided for hours towards the east. She felt weary and her head bobbed, nearly falling asleep, only to catch herself and look up. Eventually, she slept, her head resting on her hand on the canoe's edge.

A horn sounded, once then twice. Vera slowly opened her eyes, adjusting to the daylight. She was lying in the bottom of a boat. She looked around. It was the same panga as before. The motor hung lifeless on the back of the boat. There was no sign of the brothers or the canoe. To her right, she saw a large, canopied fishing boat, twenty-five feet away. Men were yelling to her from the deck. She managed to lift an arm and wave. "I'm here!" She rasped.

They threw her a line and pulled her towards them. She haltingly climbed the ladder, which felt impossibly steep, and stood on the deck. They crowded around her, asking questions.

"May I have some water?" she asked. Her cracked lips made it impossible to smile. She reached up to push back her hair, wincing as her hand touched the wound on her head. Then, surprisingly, her hand reached the back of her head, and felt two long braids, one on the left, one on the right. *Had her visitation with Mictecacihuatl been real?* Suddenly, she was dizzy. Two of the passengers reached out to grab her as she collapsed on the deck.

Vera tugged on the starched sheets of her bed. She felt exposed. Several people were crowded into the small hospital room. Her boss, Carlos Fuentes, was closest. Behind him were officers Hernandez and Gato. A nurse entered and maneuvered around the men to her bed.

"How are you feeling?" The nurse asked.

"Okay, I guess. Where am I?" Vera asked.

Fuentes spoke first. "You're back in Mexico City at Hospital Médica Sur. The fishing boat dropped you at the port in Guaymas and we airlifted you here. That was yesterday. You'd been missing for five days. We were worried."

Vera looked at the nurse. "What's my medical condition?"

"You had a serious concussion, dehydration and hypothermia. We've been giving you fluids for the past twenty-four hours. You didn't eat much, if anything, over the previous five days."

"When can I leave?"

"Whenever you're up to it," the nurse replied. "I'll do my rounds then we can go over the discharge papers." She left the room and the three men pressed closer.

"A lot has happened," Fuentes said.

She told them about her meeting with Cyclops. They discussed the implications.

Vera was suddenly very tired. “The whole thing sounds like a bad piece of fiction,” she murmured. Her eyes closed.

The three men soon left the hospital.

She slept for several hours. It was early evening when she opened her eyes. Juan Escribo was sitting in a chair, a book on his lap.

“Juan?”

His head jerked up. “Yeah?” he muttered. “Oh, I must have dozed-off.”

“No problem,” she said. “How’d you find me?”

“Your secretary told me. What happened?”

She described her encounter with the one-eyed man, being marooned like a castaway, finding the island, talking with Mictecacihuatl and being rescued.

“Do you think you actually had an encounter with the Aztec goddess of death?” Escribo asked, humorously.

“It felt real at the time. She even braided my hair. The whole experience was odd. The heavy fog, the island, the canoe ride, the brothers, it was dreamlike. They say I had a concussion and was dehydrated so who knows.”

“Where was the island?”

“She called it the Isla de los Muertos.”

“I haven’t heard of it,” Escribo said, looking thoughtful. He knew about the legend of Mictecacihuatl, who normally governed the underworld, but sometimes appeared among the living, especially on the Día de los Muertos. “She supposedly has the power to refuse a death if she believes the person's purpose in life had not been satisfied."

"Let's talk about something else," Vera said, feeling anxious. She was having trouble reconciling the experience with reality. The braids bothered her, since she'd never worn braids since childhood, and would have been unlikely to braid her own hair while lying unconscious in a boat.

Vera was suddenly dizzy. "Do you mind finding the nurse? I feel strange."

That was the last thing she recalled of her conversation in the hospital. There had been a long darkness after that.

She awoke in the bottom of a small panga boat. It offered no protection against the afternoon sun. She could hear water lapping against the metal hull, otherwise, it was quiet. She ran her hand over her head. Her straight black hair hung limply against her back.

A horn sounded, once then twice. Her father's voice was calling, *Mija, despiértete! Wake up!*

"I'm here!" she cried.

NIGHT GOBLINS

James W. Poindexter

Methought I heard a voice cry, 'Sleep no more!
Macbeth does murder sleep' - the innocent sleep,
Sleep that knits up the ravelled sleeve of care,
The death of each day's life, sore labor's bath,
Balm of hurt minds, great nature's second course,
Chief nourisher in life's feast, -
[Macbeth, Act 2, Scene 2]

Betty Faith was flailing. The sheets, like tentacles of a great sea monster, had wound around her ankles. Her face pressed down against her pillow. She managed a muffled scream, then she awoke.

Betty didn't remember the scream, or the dream that had prompted it. She was only aware of the lingering effects, the dread. *Shit!,* she thought, *I'm thirty-five years old and can't get through the night.*

She sat up. The apartment was dark. The clock said 2 a.m. The room was quiet except for her husband's snoring. He sounded like a demonic orchestra, a mixture of snorts, hums and pops. Oddly, the noise never woke *him*. She was not so lucky.

She reached for the night table and opened the small drawer. Her hand found the small pistol and rubbed its metal surface like a talisman. It was comfort enough, knowing it was there. She shut the drawer.

Bits of her dream came back to her. She'd been inside a huge concrete pipe, perhaps a water main, floating. Somebody had been with her, guiding her through the darkness. There had been creatures in the water, ready to pounce, claw or worse.

It was said that dreams were the body's way of processing the traumas of the day, but Betty thought it was the reverse. She needed the daytime to recover from the night. In her experience, most good sleepers identified themselves as either *morning persons* or *night owls*. The issue for them was not *whether* they would get the full complement of sleep, but *when*. For Betty, her circadian rhythms were a jumble, asymmetric, like dissonant jazz.

And, like other insomniacs, she had studied the subject of sleep. She was an avid reader and sleep was a worthy topic. After all, everybody did it, some better than others.

Ancient civilizations had attributed dreams to the gods. The ancient Greeks thought sleep was a form of unconsciousness brought on by lack of blood. It was not until the 19th century that scientists gave serious attention to the physiology of the brain. Basically, all animals, not just humans, needed sleep for cellular repair and restoration.

She had recently read Matthew Walker's *Why We Sleep* and Benjamin Reiss's *Wild Nights*. Before the Industrial Revolution, most people didn't sleep eight hours at a time. They slept when they could, sometimes in shifts. Some cultures even referred to a *first sleep* and a *second sleep*.

Yet, modern culture asserted an odd pressure to conform. The industrial economy required regimentation. People who slept during the day were *slothful* and people who couldn't sleep at night (about one-third of the population) were *disordered.*

Betty knew she had sleep-disorders. It was not something she could blame on her bed or external circumstances. She and her husband shared a comfortable California king. She did feel lucky not to be living in ancient times, lying on leaves, grass or animal skins. Most people, she'd learned, didn't even have a bed, as a separate piece of furniture, until the 17th century. And the concept of the bed as a personal sanctuary was very recent. Luxury models now cost as much as a car. If TV ads were any indication, the whole country was obsessed with sleep.

Yet, some great thinkers had despised sleep. Plato was definitely in that camp, describing it as: *You may as well be dead.* Edgar Allan Poe referred to sleep as *those little slices of death, how I loathe them!* Thomas Edison refused to sleep more than 4-5 hours a night. Betty would have gladly omitted the ritual altogether.

Such thoughts were not helping. She inserted her ear buds, picked up her phone and clicked on a new app. The icon for the *Sleep Shrink* app was a bunch of Zzzz over a sleepy face (- -). A list of options appeared on the screen:

Press 1 to hear the ocean
Press 2 to hear bird songs

Press 3 to hear our weekly podcast
Press 4 to listen to a calming speech
Press 5 to watch cats at play
Press 6 to hear jokes about sleep disorders
Press 7 to be hypnotized
Press 8 if all else fails.

Roberto, a co-worker, had told her about the app. He was, like Betty, rather sleep-averse. He had recognized her symptoms. There were telltale signs: patches under the eyes, irritability and yawning.

Roberto had said, "Betty Faith, you look like shit!"

She had giggled, rather hysterically, like the nut job in a horror movie. She had collected herself and said, "I'd look better if I could sleep."

"Have you heard of *Sleep Shrink*?" he had asked.

She hadn't. He had offered to download the app onto her phone. She watched as he did it, marveling at how readily she'd allowed him to install a random piece of software despite myriad warnings against it. *But really*, she thought, *who cares about security where sleep is involved.*

"Try it," he had encouraged, "it worked for me."

She had smiled. His words had given her hope.

"Oh, and don't be bothered by all the questions they ask you," he had continued. "I guess it helps them tailor the app to your needs."

"What kind of questions?"

"Oh, things like positive childhood memories, favorite birds, stuff like that. They even ask for a favorite movie. I told them mine was *The Thin Man*."

"One of my favorites too," she had said. "You can't go wrong with Nick and Nora Charles in Manhattan, drinking martinis and solving a murder."

That conversation with Roberto had been just hours earlier. She had spent some time that evening setting up the *Sleep Shrink* app. Now, here she was, eyes open, in the middle of the night. She was desperate.

She pressed option 1 on the *Sleep Shrink* app. She could hear the ocean over her ear buds. Breakers were landing on a beach and receding, *crash* then *whoosh.* Sea gulls squawked in the background. She recalled a childhood vacation at Newport Beach. Her mother looking so tan, her father commuting in the Ford Galaxy to his LA office. She had spent the vacation lounging on the beach, accompanied by the sound of the ocean, *crash* and *whoosh.* As she listened, sleep finally swept over her and pulled her under.

Betty could usually *fall* to sleep. Her problem was *staying* asleep. She woke most nights, lying there for hours. Remedies abounded. She had tried meditation, yoga, therapy and occasional breaks from alcohol and coffee.

She had taken medications, but pills made her groggy the next day. The number of pharmacological remedies for sleeplessness was staggering. The drug companies had come a long way from the early 1900s when they had first offered a barbiturate, Barbital, as a sleep aid and created a whole generation of addicts.

The following night, Betty fell asleep quickly, even before her husband, Greg, had begun to snore. Her slumber was short-lived. She woke at 12:30, unsure why.

She lay there for several minutes before putting in her ear buds and opening the *Sleep Shrink* app. She chose option 2 - *bird calls*. The mockingbird's song was so tranquil. It reminded her of long ago summers when birdsong pierced the early morning air. The mockingbird's repertoire served its purpose and lulled her back to sleep.

For years, Betty had relied on NPR radio and later podcasts to fill the empty nighttime hours. They diverted her from her own rumination. On a typical night, she might hear a succession of radio shows: one-o'clock *The beavertail cactus can survive extreme desert heat...*, one-thirty *Picasso's time in Paris was important to the development of his technique...*, two o'clock, *The history of the Inquisition in Mexico began in the sixteenth century...* The next morning, she would arrive at work *exhausted*, yet often more knowledgeable.

From Betty's point of view, pundits who warned *don't take your devices to bed* were idiots. It was no accident that people now filled their bedrooms with TVs, radios, laptops and phones.

Betty had a demanding job as media director for a congresswoman, Rep. Sandy Catalan, who was widely known as the *Sandcat*. Betty had heard that sand cats were aggressive carnivores that lived in the Sahara. The name fit. Her boss had a knack for making enemies. Fortunately, the congresswoman's district preferred a *good fight* over *good legislation*.

Outside her own district, the Sandcat was seen as a loud-mouth who catered mainly to her wealthy donors. The Sandcat's latest project was a *national vagrancy law*. Her plan was to put the homeless in jail. As media director, Betty had to explain such proposals to the public.

The goal was to make the Sandcat appear *strong,* but not so strong as to appear a *lunatic*. That was not always an easy row to hoe.

Betty never blamed her insomnia on her work. Yes, there was the constant pressure. And yes, the job compelled her to use various forms of propaganda, fake news, spin, gaslighting, false flags and slander. But that was the job. Betty's sleep disorders, on the other hand, felt more personal, like a defect in her DNA.

Still, she despised her boss, but consoled herself with the thought that *lots of people hate their bosses*.

Nor did she blame her insomnia on her husband. Certainly, he snored like a razorback. Her sleep problems, however, had preceded their marriage. She had never fully committed to the idea of marriage. She had kept her maiden name rather than become Mrs. Gregory Holmes. *Betty Holmes* sounded about as exciting as shredded wheat. She had opted *to keep the Faith*, as she had joked with her father on her wedding day.

The nights came and went, like a parade of horribles. One night, Betty dreamed that she lived in a crowded tenement building. Every time she returned home, she'd have to climb several flights, pass through turnstiles and answer questions posed by faceless figures. She had to traverse this gauntlet to reach her bedroom and, unless she reached the bedroom, she could not sleep.

She woke suddenly at 2 a.m. The dream left her exhausted. Her husband was, as usual, snoring. She got out of bed and walked to the bathroom. She paused in front of the mirror. The nightlight gave her a spectral glow. She could barely make out her features: dark hair pulled back, oversized eyes, a plain nose and a wide mouth. The image was clown-like, and somewhat sinister.

What was the point? she thought. The cycle of night and day, dreams and work, she wasn't sure what it all meant. There was always the gun in the drawer, although she had seldom thought about using it on herself.

Staring into the mirror, she remembered Hamlet's speech: *To die, to sleep – to sleep, perchance to dream. Ay, there's the rub.* What if, instead of peaceful slumber, death were a procession of nightmares? *Yes, there's the rub*, she thought.

She returned to the bedroom. It seemed unchanged, except the room was quiet. Her husband had stopped snoring. In fact, it seemed he had stopped breathing, but he soon gasped, sputtered and returned to snoring. She had encouraged him to see if he had *sleep apnea*, but he had refused to be tested.

She reached for her phone and pressed the *Sleep Shrink* app. She considered option 3, but she was weary of podcasts. Instead, she pushed option 4, *a calming speech.*

"I'm professor Lucy," the speaker intoned, in a sweet voice, not unlike a Disney princess. "Let's talk about a *forest stream.* Imagine the water moving through hillsides under a cover of fir trees. It jostles over boulders and cascades into a dark pool. The water is frothy white. The splash radiates across the pool, eventually reaching a pebbled beach. A deer and her fawns are resting there, sipping the cool water." The speech droned on. Betty was soon asleep.

Before getting her Masters in Communications, Betty had been a philosophy major at Dartmouth. Looking back at the experience, she could now imagine a professor expounding on the topic of insomnia: *Consciousness is certainly evidence of life. Should we therefore consider sleep and other unconscious states as evidence of death?* That was the kind of sophistry one discussed in college. She didn't miss it.

She had educated herself about sleep disorders. She had even spent a week at the *Stanford Sleep Academy*, which was a sort of boot camp for insomniacs. At the Academy, the somnologists had used monitors to record data and instructed the *students* on various sleep-techniques.

Betty's form of insomnia, *primary insomnia,* occurred on its own with no other co-existing disease, pain or depression. Whatever the label, *her* insomnia was real. She kept a log and made nightly entries.

René Descartes might have assessed her condition as *non dormio, ergo sum - I don't sleep, therefore I am*. Unlike Plato, Descartes had appreciated a good night's sleep. He viewed it as a gateway to the imagination: *Asleep we can imagine ourselves possessed of another body and see other stars and another earth, when there is nothing of the kind.*

"Betty, wake up!"

Betty opened her eyes. Her husband, Greg, was hovering above her, pushing the edge of the bed. The mattress was rocking like a dinghy in a typhoon. "What's happening?" she rasped. Her throat felt dry.

"You've overslept."

She turned to the clock. It said 8:30. "Greg, why didn't you wake me?"

Greg seemed bored. "Not my problem."

"You think I like it?" She said, pitifully. "Nights are a living hell for me."

Greg glanced impatiently at his watch. He was tired of the whole *sleep-drama thing*. "I called your office and told them you were sick."

"You did *what*?" She couldn't believe it. She wasn't some slouch who could beg off work any time she had a splinter. Her job *mattered.*

"Whatever," he said, indifferently. "I have an open house over in Brentwood." He left the room.

She heard the front door shut. Greg was off to his endless parade of open houses, not to mention cute trainees accumulating hours for their agent's license. Betty had never owned a home. She preferred to rent. *Who needed termites, leaky roofs and mortgages?*

Three years of marriage and their relationship already felt stale. Greg didn't *get* her. He ridiculed her insomnia as a trivial thing, like a passing case of acne. Her sleeplessness defined her. *If he didn't understand that,* she thought, *then he couldn't understand me.* And, to complete the thought, *if he didn't understand me, how could he love me*?

Betty had gone to work anyway. She went to the Sandcat's office to apologize. It felt odd offering an apology for sleeping too much. In Mediterranean cultures, like Spain and Greece, the goal had traditionally been to get a decent night's sleep, then top it off with a siesta. *I would have fit into that system*, she thought, *making up in the day what you lost at night*. She had remembered an *interesting fact*: Greece had recently abandoned the siesta and, as a result, heart disease had increased nearly forty percent.

The Sandcat was angry. “You know, Betty, you can’t just come to work whenever the mood suits you!”

“Of course,” Betty said, feigning contrition. “It won’t happen again.”

“Damn right!” the Sandcat crowed. “I want you to focus on promoting the anti-vagrancy bill. The *hobo-huggers* are turning the media against us. The public spaces are for the taxpaying public, not the *housing disadvantaged* or whatever they call themselves these days!”

Betty thought about quitting. And she might have, if it wouldn’t have meant relying on Greg to pay the rent. “I’ll get on it,” she said, without enthusiasm, as she left the office.

In the hallway, Betty nearly bumped into Roberto. His smile was the first bright spot of the day.

“What’s the rush?” he asked.

“Oh, I was late to work and the Sandcat’s pissed.”

“You know, I was a private-eye back in the day,” he said, trying to lighten the mood.

“And so?” she said, impatiently.

“Well, I can tell you’re a bit out of sorts. Isn’t the *Sleep Shrink* app doing the job?”

She didn’t want to get into it. “Yeah, the app’s fine, I guess. It’s everything else.”

A few nights later, Betty had an especially bad night. She dreamed that she was a child, abandoned on a city street. She was cold and alone. She woke to a serenade of snorts and whistles, her husband’s snoring. The *Sleep Shrink* app had, by now, become habit. She seized her phone.

She tried option 5 - *watch cats play*. The cats were cute and funny, but the videos were hardly restful. They felt edited. *Could a cat really play violin?*

She moved on to option 6 - *insomnia jokes*. Some of the humor was amusing. Have you seen *Insomnia*, the horror movie? *Yeah, I couldn't sleep for days*. What do you call a sleepwalking nun? *A roamin' Catholic*. Would you like some advice about insomnia? *Maybe, but I'll have to sleep on it.* If there's a queen size and a king size mattress, where does the prince sleep? *On an heir mattress*. I hear you're really good at sleeping? *Yeah, I can do it with my eyes closed.* Do you want to volunteer for our sleep study? *Sure, that's my dream job*.

Weirdly, the jokes made her feel like she was part of something. There were tons of insomniacs, over a hundred million in the U. S. The condition was so common, they had written thousands of jokes about it.

However, the jokes were not working. She was still wide awake. She moved on to option 7 - *hypnosis*. A man's voice, deep and confident, said, "Hi Betty, thank you for calling in tonight."

Betty was suddenly alert. "How do you know my name?"

There was a pause. "Betty, let's focus on *you*. Can we do that?"

She assumed the algorithm within the *Sleep Shrink* app had gotten her name from the client information when she had downloaded the app. Still, it felt a bit intrusive. "Yes, okay," she said, reluctantly.

"I'm starting a metronome," the voice said, "to set a tempo. It will help pace our conversation." A gentle *tick tock* repeated in the background. It sounded like a grandfather's clock. "Betty, please shut your eyes," the voice said, soothingly.

"Okay," she said, slowly.

"Clear your mind. Just focus on my voice."

The next morning, she couldn't remember what had happened. She looked at her watch which, among its many practical uses, measured the time she spent asleep (Deep, Core, REM) and awake. The up and down lines on the chart looked like a seismograph during a major quake. However, around the time of the hypnosis, the chart showed that she had drifted into a lengthy and deep sleep.

A deep sleep so rarely happened to her. It was the feeling of time passing without knowing it. She had read David Hume in college. He had said, *A man asleep is insensible of time*. She had met people like that. They said things like, *Oh, I sleep through the night, doesn't everybody?* It was a useful distinction between good and bad sleepers. The former rested, unconscious of time, while the others flitted from dream, to consciousness, to fitful sleep, waiting for dawn.

Sleep Shrink's hypnosis option had helped. Betty felt more rested. She even had a few good days at work. Despite the Sandcat's mood swings, Betty remained unfazed and had even told some sleep jokes to her co-workers, who were pleasantly surprised. One had said, "Whoa, what's gotten into Betty?" Another had said, "Yeah, she's weirdly fun, today."

For several nights, Betty used the hypnosis option. It seemed to be working. She rarely got very far into the program before she was sound asleep. And, the next day, she had little memory of what had been said.

One night, she was especially stressed out. She took a sleeping pill and had what she thought was an odd dream. She grabbed the pistol from her drawer and left the apartment, taking the stairs down to the building lobby. For some reason, the elevator was not working.

The security man at the lobby desk asked, "Are you alright, Miss?"

"Oh, yes, I'm just going out for milk," she answered.

"Maybe the bodega on the corner is still open," the guard said, helpfully.

She passed through the glass door on to the street. It had been raining. The streetlights glistened off of parked cars and building windows. She then realized that she was in her bathrobe and slippers. Nobody was on the street. She kept walking. The corner bodega, however, was closed. Across the street, she saw a brightly lit Dunkin' Donuts. She crossed the street and entered. The glare from the fluorescent lighting was nearly blinding.

"Can I help you?" the counterman asked. He didn't seem to notice she was in her bathrobe.

"May I have a dozen old fashioned and a glass of milk?"

The counterman poured her a glass of milk, which she promptly drank. He then picked up an orange and pink box and started filling it.

She reached into her bathrobe pocket for her wallet. It was empty except for a used tissue. She tried the other pocket and felt something metallic and cold. She pulled out her .22 pistol.

The counterman turned toward her. "What the hell, lady!"

"I'll take those donuts," she said, now pointing the gun at him.

He handed her the box and backed away. She crammed two of the donuts into her mouth, closed the box and left. As she stepped onto the sidewalk, two patrol cops approached. She pocketed the gun and began walking away. The cops didn't pay her much attention. They were accustomed to odd things at night, especially at a donut shop.

By now, the counterman was yelling, "She has a gun! She didn't pay for the donuts!"

She ran up the sidewalk and turned left into a dark alley. There were puddles in potholes. She tried to step around them. She moved past dumpsters and gray buildings. A man, standing to one side of the alley, called out, "Hold it lady!" She slowed. The man was bulky, in a blue sweatshirt. He had a red beard. More significantly, he held a knife. "Give me your money!" he ordered.

"What money?"

He grabbed her shoulder and patted her down. "What's this?" he asked, pulling the gun from her bathrobe. He stared at the box in her hand. "And I'll take those," he said, grabbing the donuts.

She was running. She glanced back and saw the cops entering the alley. Red-beard was gone.

Betty woke the next morning, feeling queasy. She couldn't remember what she had eaten the night before. Her lips tasted sugary, like donuts. She got out of bed. For some reason, her bathrobe was on the chair and not in the closet where she normally kept it. And her slippers felt clammy.

Throughout that week, Betty continued to have vivid dreams, which she dutifully recorded in her log. In one dream, her mother was offering advice about finding a better husband. In another, the Sandcat had turned up naked at a rally, having promised to *bare all in order to make government more transparent*. In another, plants and animals spoke to her, complaining that *homo sapiens* had ruined the planet. *Yikes!* she had written in her log, *is everyone this fucked up?!*

She was having trouble distinguishing dreams from reality. They felt lifelike.

A few nights later, Betty and Greg had gone to a neighbor's for dinner. They had some red wine, oysters and chocolate mousse. She knew the combination would be a problem. Later that night, she woke abruptly at 2:00 a.m. feeling anxious.

It was probably the food, she thought. Thomas Hobbes, the political philosopher, had been interested in sleep. He believed that *dreams are caused by the distemper of some inward parts of the Body*. Her stomach was evidently experiencing something akin to *distemper*.

She was having trouble controlling her anxiety. Her watch, which she had worn to bed, started chiming. The screen showed the image of a pulsing heart. Her heart rate was spiking. *I need to calm down*, she thought. Panic attacks in the dead of night were never a good thing. One disquieting thought was leading to another. She reached for her phone. Hypnosis seemed inadequate. She decided to try option 8 - *if all else fails*.

At first, nothing happened. A wheel spun on the screen, downloading. It then said, *You have chosen a premium service. There is a one-time charge of $500. How do you wish to pay?*

What the fuck? Betty thought, feeling the blood rush to her temples. *Do I have a choice?* She entered her Apple ID and she was in.

"Hi Betty, this is William Powell," the voice said over the phone.

“Like the old-time movie star?” she asked, feeling jittery.

“Sort of, I *am* rather tall, dark and handsome.”

“Are you an AI or a real person?” she asked, thinking there should be a Turing test for this.

“Does it matter?” the voice responded.

Betty thought about it. It was such a muddle. She supposed they had used the name William Powell since he had played Nick Charles in *The Thin Man*. “I guess it doesn’t matter,” she replied, feeling a bit calmer. “What can you do for me?”

“I’m going to pose some questions,” William Powell said. He then asked her about her marriage, her job, her hobbies, her reading, what made her feel good or bad. She typed in her answers, not wanting to risk waking her husband.

“Betty, it sounds like your marriage is not very satisfying.”

“Maybe, but I hate living alone.”

“Not much of a reason for being married,” he said.

For the next few nights, she and William Powell chatted via *Sleep Shrink*’s option 8. She shared a great deal of personal information. She wasn’t too worried about it, since the app had promised *strict confidentiality*. William Powell would end each call by telling her a pleasant story and she would fall asleep.

One day, her co-worker, Roberto, asked her to lunch. He appeared nervous, which was unusual for him. He was normally unflustered and matter of fact. He had previously been a private detective, but was now reduced to performing background checks for the congresswoman. Betty agreed to meet him at the Timberlake Bar.

They sat at a booth and ordered lunch. “What’s up, Roberto.”

He had lost weight and seemed troubled. “I shouldn’t have told you about *Sleep Shrink*.”

He sounded a little loopy. She waited for him to compose himself.

“There’s something about that app,” he continued.

“How’s that?”

“I think it rewires your brain, makes it hard to tell what’s real and what isn’t.”

This sounded like tinfoil hat stuff. Then she thought about her own dreams. They were getting harder to distinguish from actual events. “Yeah, I guess, I’ve noticed that.”

Roberto continued. “But option 8 is even weirder. That option put me in touch with somebody called *Myrna Loy*.”

Betty looked surprised. “That’s strange” she replied, “option 8 connected me to *William Powell*.” She laughed, feeling uneasy. She was starting to sense they were *inside* a Dashiell Hammett novel. “Maybe, it makes sense since we both said *The Thin Man* was our favorite movie."

Roberto sighed. “Most nights, I look forward to talking with Myrna Loy.” He smiled, a little sheepishly. “It’s like that movie *Her*, where Joaquin Phoenix falls in love with his smart phone. Myrna understands me.”

Betty felt the same about William Powell. She was losing her fear of going to bed. He was a pleasant alternative to night sweats. Despite odd dreams, and late night conversations with a robot/man named William Powell, she was convinced that *things were looking up!*

Then, the Honorable Sandy Catalan was gunned down in her office.

Betty was at work at the time. There was a loud *bang!* A few moments later, somebody yelled, “Help! The Sandcat’s been shot!”

The police arrived. They found the murder weapon, a small caliber gun, in the congresswoman’s office. They took statements from Betty, Roberto and the other employees. Nobody had witnessed the actual shooting.

It was assumed that somebody had entered the office from the street. Perhaps, they speculated, it had been a homeless person upset with the Sandcat’s stance on the vagrancy bill.

The congresswoman never regained consciousness. She died on her way to the hospital.

Despite the Sandcat’s death, there was still work to do. The Governor planned to appoint a replacement until a special election could be held. The Sandcat’s records had to be logged and accounts settled. Employees, who were willing to do so, could remain on the payroll during the transition.

A week later, Betty and Roberto were seated at a conference room table, reviewing some of the Sandcat’s files. Two men in coats and ties entered the room.

“Excuse me,” the taller man said, “are you Betty Faith?”

Betty looked up from the pile of papers. “Yes, that’s me. Who are you?”

“I’m Detective Marvin Willis and he’s Donny Webb,” Willis said, pointing at his partner. “We’ve traced the gun that was used in the shooting. It was a Smith & Wesson .22 subcompact pistol. Sound familiar?”

Betty started to shake her head.

Roberto stood up. "Why are you asking her all these questions?"

"The gun was found at the scene. It was registered to Ms. Faith's husband, Greg Holmes. He has a different last name so it took us a while to make the connection to Betty."

Betty was now staring up at Roberto. "None of this makes sense," she said, confused.

Detective Willis gestured for her to stand. "Sorry, but you'll have to come with us. We need a formal statement from you."

The following day, Betty and Roberto were sitting on stools at the Timberlake Bar. They ordered Martinis. The drink seemed appropriate, like a scene from the *Thin Man*, Nick and Nora Charles on Christmas holiday in New York City. The bartender set down two napkins, their drinks and a bowl of nuts.

"So what happened at the police station?" Roberto asked.

"They asked me all about the gun. I usually keep it in the drawer by the bed. Obviously, it wasn't there when I checked last night."

"So what happened to it?" Roberto asked, looking perplexed.

"Well, that's a problem." Betty said, "A while back, I had a dream, or what I thought was a dream, that I'd robbed some donuts from a Dunkin' Donuts at gunpoint. But, I was later assaulted by a guy in an alley who took the donuts and my gun."

Roberto shook his head, bewildered. "What? So, it wasn't a dream?"

"I don't know," she said, shakily, "I'm frightened."

"What *do* you remember?"

"It sounds lame. I took a sleeping pill so I'm not really sure. But it's the only way to explain how the gun could have ended up in the Sandcat's office. I didn't put it there!" she said, her voice rising.

"So, you don't have an alibi? Nobody to say where you were at the time of the shooting?"

"No. I remember being alone when I heard the shot."

"Take it easy," he said. "I'm sure they'll figure it out."

A few minutes passed. They sipped their cocktails.

"Is it just me?" he asked, trying to lighten the conversation, "or is this bar starting to look like the Blue Bar at the Algonquin Hotel?"

She hadn't really noticed.

"Look at the furniture, the fixtures," Roberto said. "It resembles the Blue Bar when it opened near Times Square at the end of Prohibition in 1933."

"Right," said Betty, grateful for the change in topic, "That was the year before Hammett published the *Thin Man* and the movie came out." She was a big fan of Dashiell Hammett. "Hammett wrote it while he and Lillian Hellman were living at the Sutton Hotel on East 56th Street."

"Yeah, they were *the* literary power couple."

She was now taking a closer look at Roberto. He usually wore khakis and a polo shirt. Today he was dressed in a gray double-breasted suit, striped tie and gray fedora. He had a trench coat slung over the chair. "You look different. Kind of like Nick Charles. What's the occasion?"

"Nothing really," Roberto said, blushing, "Just felt like dressing up. What's your excuse?"

Betty had always liked vintage clothes, but rarely wore them to work. She had decided to wear a belted, calf-length, A-line dress with puff sleeves. "Maybe, this *Thin Man* thing *is* affecting us," she said.

"Maybe," Roberto agreed, archly.

Just then, a small white dog ran into the bar. A city worker followed, in hot pursuit. The dog ran under the stool where Betty was sitting.

"Excuse me," the city worker called out, "I'm with Animal Control. I'll get that dog."

The dog, a wire-haired fox terrier, had other plans. He looked a lot like Skippy, who played Asta in the *Thin Man* movie. He crouched behind Betty's shoes and began barking.

Now, now, enough of that!" said the man from Animal Control, stooping closer with his pole and net.

The dog, plainly in fear, looked up at Betty and began whining.

"Look, Roberto, it's Asta," Betty said. "He's so cute!"

With that, the dog leaped upward, landing on Betty's lap. His short tail wagged. He stood on his hind legs and licked her face.

Animal Control moved in ominously. "Give 'im over, lady," he demanded.

Betty stood, holding the dog. She glanced at Roberto, gave him an *Oh well* gesture, then took off running toward the exit. "Shit," she yelled, half way across the bar, realizing that she was wearing heels.

Animal Control was on the heavy side and was slow to react. Roberto grabbed the man's net. The man then had to decide whether to drop the pole and chase Betty or stay and confront Roberto. He opted for the latter, after all the pole was city property and his responsibility. "Hey buddy, let go!"

Roberto's hand was now enmeshed in the net. "Hang on!" he yelled, "I'm trying to get out of this thing." He spent a minute clumsily attempting to free himself. "Okay, it's all yours."

Meanwhile, the officer said, "Who was that lady, what's her name and address?"

"Hell if I know," Roberto confided, "I was just trying to pick her up. Didn't get very far."

The officer looked at the bartender who merely shrugged.

"God, this job sucks sometimes," Animal Control muttered and left.

That night, Betty tried to explain to Greg why there was a dog in their apartment. He was uninterested. "He can stay tonight, but tomorrow you get rid of him. Dogs are dirty."

The dog spent a comfortable night on the bed. Betty, however, was unable to sleep, thinking about the possibility of her imminent arrest.

Betty showed up to work the next day, accompanied by the dog, whom she introduced as Asta. She wasted no time finding Roberto. "I couldn't sleep last night," she said.

He looked at her, indifferently. "Yeah, so."

"I know, so what's new, right?" she said, "but I think they're going to blame me for the Sandcat's murder. How else do you explain my gun being there? I have no alibi and I'm worried they won't buy my Dunkin' Donuts story. It sounds bogus, even to me."

He nodded. "So, what can we do about it?"

She had decided during the night that they should solve the Sandcat's murder. "C'mon Roberto. The police are clueless. I need your help. Let's find out who shot the boss."

"Whoa, I gave up my PI license years ago. Now, I just dig up dirt on the Sandcat's enemies. Or at least I did."

"Look, we're unemployed and have free time. And you were once a *real* detective."

He was about to say no, but then reconsidered. He enjoyed being with Betty. This might give him an excuse. "Well, maybe."

"Where do we start?" she asked, enthusiastically.

The next few days moved quickly. Roberto and Betty, accompanied by Asta, interviewed their co-workers. The congresswoman's office manager, Mary Hamstead, had heard the shot but had not seen the assailant. The CCTV footage had been similarly vague.

They also reviewed the Sandcat's correspondence. There was a large folder of hate mail. Most of the threats related to the Sandcat's proposed vagrancy law.

They cautiously approached Detective Marvin Willis, who was heading the police investigation. According to Willis, fingerprints, carpet fibers, gunshot residue, and ballistics had been analyzed. No positive matches were found, except that the bullet and shell casing were believed to be from the Smith & Wesson .22LR subcompact pistol. They had interviewed Betty's husband Greg, but he had been at an open house at the time of the murder. That left Betty as the most likely suspect. Willis was candid, they were close to arresting her. He just needed the District Attorney's approval.

"What about the Dunkin' Donuts theory?" Roberto asked.

Willis shrugged. "You really want us using City resources on a *dream*, about robbing a box of donuts and then being assaulted in an alley, while wearing her bathrobe and slippers?"

"Did you find anything else?" Betty asked, nervously, trying to change the subject.

"Well, among the collected fibers, we found *a single red hair.*"

Betty and Roberto returned to the Timberlake Bar to discuss what they'd learned.

"A single red hair," Roberto said, taking a sip of beer.

"Willis said it didn't have a root, so no DNA," Betty added. "What about the political angle?"

"Well, let's assume your imagined guy in the alley was pissed off about the vagrancy bill. Maybe he was homeless."

"Does that make sense?" she asked. "I mean a guy in an alley happens to steal my gun and, coincidentally, he's hell bent on murdering my boss over her legislative policies. Kind of a stretch, no?"

"Yeah, it really sounds like a dream," he agreed.

"More like a nightmare."

Betty went home that night, rather disheartened. They weren't making any progress solving the murder. Beyond that, she hadn't made any headway finding Asta a proper home. If she was arrested, who knew what Greg would do with the dog, probably just leave him on the street.

Greg was at the apartment when she arrived. "Goddammit, Betty," he said, as soon as she walked in. "You know I don't like dogs. They smell. You have to walk them, and carry those little bags of poop. It's gross!"

He had finished off most of a bottle of Zinfandel. There was no point in reasoning with him. "Let's talk about it tomorrow. I need some sleep," Betty said, waving her hand, then disappearing into the bedroom.

"That Detective Willis thinks you killed your boss," Greg shouted after her.

She took two sleeping pills. She just wanted to get through the night. She fell asleep thinking about the *single red hair*.

It was well known that Zolpidem can cause sleepwalking. A person may remember it as a dream, with no memory of having left the bed.

The next morning, Betty learned that she had been found after midnight, scantily dressed in the building lobby. According to the night guard, she kept repeating that she *had to find the man with the red beard who had the gun*. The guard had called up to Greg who, after ten rings, had finally picked up the phone.

After Greg went off to work, Betty dressed quickly and called Roberto. "Meet me at the donut shop across the street from my building."

"Why now?" Roberto asked.

"You'll see."

The images from her dream flooded her mind. Her waking life and dreams, once oil and water, were coalescing, weaving together like a piece of fabric.

She and Asta walked along the sidewalk. She saw the bodega on the corner, which was now open. And there, across the street, was the Dunkin' Donuts. And beyond there, she could see a dark, narrow alley.

She entered the donut shop.

"Sorry, Miss, no dogs allowed."

"Really, he's a service dog. I can't sleep without him," she explained.

"Well, you can't sleep here either."

"Just give me a coffee, please, then I'll go."

She took the coffee outside and waited.

Roberto arrived soon. He patted Asta on the head, "How's it going, boy." Asta wagged his tail. Roberto looked up at Betty. "So why are we here?"

She told him about what she had thought was a dream: wandering out in her bathrobe, stealing the donuts at gun point, the cops, being confronted in the alley and *red-beard* taking the gun and donuts. She asked, "What if the dream was like a premonition or some kind of parallel universe?"

Roberto shrugged. "Or maybe it wasn't a dream. Maybe it really happened." He could see that Betty was disconcerted. "Well, let's look in the alley. It could trigger a memory."

Meanwhile, the donut shop clerk had been eyeing Betty. He was making a call. She could see him, speaking adamantly into the phone, as she and Roberto walked half a block and turned into the alley. The daylight barely penetrated the narrow lane. Signs on both sides said *No Parking*. About midway up the alley, they saw a man in a blue sweatshirt lying on a silver tarp, tucked part way behind a dumpster.

"Oh, my God, that's him!" Betty exclaimed.

"Who?"

"The red-bearded man from my dream. He took my gun!"

The man was surprisingly agile. He stood upright and pulled a knife from his jacket. He waved the knife threateningly at them.

Asta started snarling and pulling against the leash.

Red-beard was raising the knife, when a voice called out near the alley's entrance. "Hey, hold it there! Police!"

Red-beard turned. At that moment, Roberto reached for red-beard's arm. The knife grazed Roberto's forearm then fell to the ground. Two uniformed police ran towards them.

Betty was in shock. "He had a knife," she said, bending down to reach for it.

"Hey, don't touch that," one of the cops shouted.

Roberto had remained calm. "You should call Detective Marvin Willis. We think this guy might be the one who killed Congresswoman Catalan."

"The Catalan killing? Really?"

Detective Willis arrived and took charge. The EMTs bandaged Roberto's arm and red-beard was taken into custody. For the moment, the only charges were for assault.

Within a few hours, they matched the single red hair to the man's beard. Soon after, red-beard launched into a political rant and confessed to the killing.

Betty and Roberto later met with Detective Willis at the police station.

"Why did he do it?" asked Betty.

"He was angry about the congresswoman's plan to put homeless people in jail," Detective Willis replied. "He's still spouting off about that."

"There's too much hate in the world," Roberto mused.

"Tell me about it," agreed the detective. "And Betty, Dunkin' Donuts is willing to forego the armed robbery charge *if* you pay for the dozen donuts you took. They understand you were sleepwalking."

"Of course, thanks. What about the gun?" Betty asked.

"We'll have to keep it as evidence, at least for now."

That night, Betty told Greg what had happened.

"I guess you really did sleep walk to Dunkin' Donuts," Greg said. That was all he could muster. Given the harrowing events of the day, he was willing to allow Asta to spend one more night in the apartment. "But, tomorrow, he goes!"

Betty said she was tired and went to bed. Asta curled up by her feet. Just before falling asleep, she deleted the *Sleep Shrink* app from her phone. *I'm ready to move on*, she thought.

Around one a.m., there was a pounding on the apartment's door. *Bang, bang, bang.* Betty woke. Greg was snoring. She put on a bathrobe and slippers and walked through the dark apartment to the door. Asta stood warily behind her.

She saw Roberto through the peep hole. She opened the door slightly.

"I couldn't sleep," he said.

"Why not?" she asked.

Roberto looked forlorn. “I realized that, now the case is solved, I won’t see you every day.”

She undid the latch and opened the door wider. “Would you consider working nights?” she asked, now facing him. “I’m thinking of taking a night shift.”

“Of course,” he said and, without hesitating, added. “I love you.”

“Give me a minute,” she said. She went into the apartment and returned, dressed and holding a small travel bag. She handed Roberto the leash and Asta wagged his tail.”

“Darling,” Betty said, with a wide smile, “I’m ready!”

Roberto smiled. It was like a scene from a 1930s movie. “You’re beautiful!” he said.

As Betty was about to close the apartment door, Greg suddenly appeared from inside. He stuck his head out the doorway. His face was heavy with sleep. “Betty? What’s going on?”

“Nothing, Greg. Go back to bed.”

Betty took Roberto’s arm and they turned towards the elevator.

Just then, a song emerged from a neighbor’s apartment. It was Bing Crosby’s 1930s hit *Our Big Love Scene*. It had played at the end of *The Thin Man.*

Betty and Roberto looked at each other.

“Do you believe in coincidences?” she asked.

“I do now!” he said, beaming.

Asta barked excitedly and leaped into Roberto’s arms.

Betty laughed. “And here’s to dreams coming true.”

Made in the USA
Middletown, DE
31 March 2025

73446627R10085